CRESSY

BRET HARTE

1st WORLD
LIBRARY
Literary Society

Cressy

Bret Harte

© 1st World Library, 2007
PO Box 2211
Fairfield, IA 52556
www.1stworldlibrary.com
First Edition

LCCN: 2007927698

Softcover ISBN: 978-1-4218-4505-0
Hardcover ISBN: 978-1-4218-4421-3
eBook ISBN: 978-1-4218-4589-0

Purchase *"Cressy"*
as a traditional bound book at:
www.1stWorldLibrary.com/purchase.asp?ISBN=978-1-4218-4505-0

1st World Library is a literary, educational organization
dedicated to:

- Creating a free internet library of downloadable ebooks

- Hosting writing competitions and offering book publishing
  scholarships.

Interested in more 1st World Library books? contact:
literacy@1stworldlibrary.com
Check us out at: www.1stworldlibrary.com

1ˢᵗ World Library Literary Society

Giving Back to the World

"If you want to work on the core problem, it's early school literacy."

- James Barksdale, former CEO of Netscape

"No skill is more crucial to the future of a child, or to a democratic and prosperous society, than literacy."

- Los Angeles Times

"Literacy... means far more than learning how to read and write... The aim is to transmit... knowledge and promote social participation."

- UNESCO

"Literacy is not a luxury, it is a right and a responsibility. If our world is to meet the challenges of the twenty-first century we must harness the energy and creativity of all our citizens."

- President Bill Clinton

"Parents should be encouraged to read to their children, and teachers should be equipped with all available techniques for teaching literacy, so the varying needs and capacities of individual kids can be taken into account."

- Hugh Mackay

CHAPTER I

As the master of the Indian Spring school emerged from the pine woods into the little clearing before the schoolhouse, he stopped whistling, put his hat less jauntily on his head, threw away some wild flowers he had gathered on his way, and otherwise assumed the severe demeanor of his profession and his mature age—which was at least twenty. Not that he usually felt this an assumption; it was a firm conviction of his serious nature that he impressed others, as he did himself, with the blended austerity and ennui of deep and exhausted experience.

The building which was assigned to him and his flock by the Board of Education of Tuolumne County, California, had been originally a church. It still bore a faded odor of sanctity, mingled, however, with a later and slightly alcoholic breath of political discussion, the result of its weekly occupation under the authority of the Board as a Tribune for the enunciation of party principles and devotion to the Liberties of the People. There were a few dog-eared hymn-books on the teacher's desk, and the blackboard but imperfectly hid an impassioned appeal to the citizens of Indian Spring to "Rally" for Stebbins as Supervisor. The master had been struck with the size of the black type in which this placard was printed, and with a shrewd perception of its value to the round wandering eyes of his smaller pupils, allowed it to remain as a pleasing example of orthography. Unfortunately, although subdivided and spelt by them in its separate letters with painful and perfect accuracy, it was collectively known as "Wally," and its general import productive of vague hilarity.

Taking a large key from his pocket, the master unlocked the door and threw it open, stepping back with a certain precaution begotten of his experience in once finding a small but sociable rattlesnake coiled up near the threshold. A slight disturbance which followed his intrusion showed the value of that precaution, and the fact that the room had been already used for various private and peaceful gatherings of animated nature. An irregular attendance of yellow-birds and squirrels dismissed themselves hurriedly through the broken floor and windows, but a golden lizard, stiffened suddenly into stony fright on the edge of an open arithmetic, touched the heart of the master so strongly by its resemblance to some kept-in and forgotten scholar who had succumbed over the task he could not accomplish, that he was seized with compunction.

Recovering himself, and re-establishing, as it were, the decorous discipline of the room by clapping his hands and saying "Sho!" he passed up the narrow aisle of benches, replacing the forgotten arithmetic, and picking up from the desks here and there certain fragmentary pieces of plaster and crumbling wood that had fallen from the ceiling, as if this grove of Academus had been shedding its leaves overnight. When he reached his own desk he lifted the lid and remained for some moments motionless, gazing into it. His apparent meditation however was simply the combined reflection of his own features in a small pocket-mirror in its recesses and a perplexing doubt in his mind whether the sacrifice of his budding moustache was not essential to the professional austerity of his countenance. But he was presently aware of the sound of small voices, light cries, and brief laughter scattered at vague and remote distances from the schoolhouse—not unlike the birds and squirrels he had just dispossessed. He recognized by these signs that it was nine o'clock, and his scholars were assembling.

They came in their usual desultory fashion—the fashion of country school-children the world over—irregularly, spasmodically, and always as if accidentally; a few hand-in-hand, others driven ahead of or dropped behind their elders; some in straggling groups more or less coherent and at times only connected by far-off intermediate voices scattered on a space of half a mile, but never quite alone; always preoccupied by something else than the actual business on hand; appearing suddenly from ditches, behind trunks, and between fence-rails; cropping up in unexpected places along the road after vague and purposeless detours—seemingly going anywhere and everywhere but to school! So unlooked-for, in fact, was their final arrival that the master, who had a few moments before failed to descry a single torn straw hat or ruined sunbonnet above his visible horizon, was always startled to find them suddenly under his windows, as if, like the birds, they had alighted from the trees. Nor was their moral attitude towards their duty any the more varied; they always arrived as if tired and reluctant, with a doubting sulkiness that perhaps afterwards beamed into a charming hypocrisy, but invariably temporizing with their instincts until the last moment, and only relinquishing possible truancy on the very threshold. Even after they were marshalled on their usual benches they gazed at each other every morning with a perfectly fresh astonishment and a daily recurring enjoyment of some hidden joke in this tremendous rencontre.

It had been the habit of the master to utilize these preliminary vagrancies of his little flock by inviting them on assembling to recount any interesting incident of their journey hither; or failing this, from their not infrequent shyness in expressing what had secretly interested them, any event that had occurred within their knowledge since they last met. He had done this, partly to give them time to recover themselves in that more formal atmosphere, and partly, I fear, because, notwithstanding his conscientious gravity, it greatly amused him. It also diverted them from their usual round-eyed, breathless contemplation of himself—a regular morning inspection which generally embraced every detail of his dress and appearance, and made every change or deviation the subject of whispered comment or stony astonishment. He knew that they knew him more thoroughly than he did himself, and shrank from the intuitive vision of these small clairvoyants.

"Well?" said the master gravely.

There was the usual interval of bashful hesitation, verging on nervous hilarity or hypocritical attention. For the last six months this question by the master had been invariably received each morning as a veiled pleasantry which might lead to baleful information or conceal some query out of the dreadful books before him. Yet this very element of danger had its fascinations. Johnny Filgee, a small boy, blushed violently, and, without getting up, began hurriedly in a high key, "Tige ith got," and then suddenly subsided into a whisper.

"Speak up, Johnny," said the master encouragingly.

"Please, sir, it ain't anythin' he's seed—nor any real news," said Rupert Filgee, his elder brother, rising with family concern and frowning openly upon Johnny; "it's jest his foolishness; he oughter be licked." Finding himself unexpectedly on his feet, and apparently at the end of a long speech, he colored also, and then said hurriedly, "Jimmy

Snyder—HE seed suthin'. Ask HIM!" and sat down—a recognized hero.

Every eye, including the master's, was turned on Jimmy Snyder. But that youthful observer, instantly diving his head and shoulders into his desk, remained there gurgling as if under water. Two or three nearest him endeavored with some struggling to bring him to an intelligible surface again. The master waited patiently. Johnny Filgee took advantage of the diversion to begin again in a high key, "Tige ith got thix," and subsided.

"Come, Jimmy," said the master, with a touch of peremptoriness. Thus adjured, Jimmy Snyder came up glowingly, and bristling with full stops and exclamation points. "Seed a black b'ar comin' outer Daves' woods," he said excitedly. "Nigh to me ez you be. 'N big ez a hoss; 'n snarlin'! 'n snappin'!—like gosh! Kem along—ker—clump torords me. Reckoned he'd skeer me! Didn't skeer me worth a cent. I heaved a rock at him—I did now!" (in defiance of murmurs of derisive comment)—"'n he slid. Ef he'd kem up furder I'd hev up with my slate and swotted him over the snoot—bet your boots!"

The master here thought fit to interfere, and gravely point out that the habit of striking bears as large as a horse with a school-slate was equally dangerous to the slate (which was also the property of Tuolumne County) and to the striker; and that the verb "to swot" and the noun substantive "snoot" were likewise indefensible, and not to be tolerated. Thus admonished Jimmy Snyder, albeit unshaken in his faith in his own courage, sat down.

A slight pause ensued. The youthful Filgee, taking advantage of it, opened in a higher key, "Tige ith"—but the master's attention was here diverted by the searching eyes of Octavia

Dean, a girl of eleven, who after the fashion of her sex preferred a personal recognition of her presence before she spoke. Succeeding in catching his eye, she threw back her long hair from her shoulders with an easy habitual gesture, rose, and with a faint accession of color said:

"Cressy McKinstry came home from Sacramento. Mrs. McKinstry told mother she's comin' back here to school."

The master looked up with an alacrity perhaps inconsistent with his cynical austerity. Seeing the young girl curiously watching him with an expectant smile, he regretted it. Cressy McKinstry, who was sixteen years old, had been one of the pupils he had found at the school when he first came. But as he had also found that she was there in the extraordinary attitude of being "engaged" to one Seth Davis, a fellow-pupil of nineteen, and as most of the courtship was carried on freely and unceremoniously during school-hours with the full permission of the master's predecessor, the master had been obliged to point out to the parents of the devoted couple the embarrassing effects of this association on the discipline of the school. The result had been the withdrawal of the lovers, and possibly the good-will of the parents. The return of the young lady was consequently a matter of some significance. Had the master's protest been accepted, or had the engagement itself been broken off?

Either was not improbable. His momentary loss of attention was Johnny Filgee's great gain.

"Tige," said Johnny, with sudden and alarming distinctness, "ith got thix pupths—mothly yaller."

In the laugh which followed this long withheld announcement of an increase in the family of Johnny's yellow and disreputable setter "Tiger," who usually accompanied him to school and howled outside, the master joined with marked distinctness. Then he said, with equally marked severity, "Books!" The little levee was ended, and school began.

It continued for two hours with short sighs, corrugations of small foreheads, the complaining cries and scratchings of slate pencils over slates, and other signs of minor anguish among the more youthful of the flock; and with more or less whisperings, movements of the lips, and unconscious soliloquy among the older pupils. The master moved slowly up and down the aisle with a word of encouragement or explanation here and there, stopping with his hands behind him to gaze abstractedly out of the windows to the wondering envy of the little ones. A faint hum, as of invisible insects, gradually pervaded the school; the more persistent droning of a large bee had become dangerously soporific. The hot breath of the pines without had invaded the doors and windows; the warped shingles and weather-boarding at times creaked and snapped under the rays of the vertical and unclouded sun. A gentle perspiration broke out like a mild epidemic in the infant class; little curls became damp, brief lashes limp, round eyes moist, and small eyelids heavy. The master himself started, and awoke out of a perilous dream of other eyes and hair to collect himself severely. For the irresolute, half-embarrassed, half-lazy figure of a man had halted doubtingly before the porch and open door. Luckily the children, who were facing the master with their backs to the entrance, did not see it.

Yet the figure was neither alarming nor unfamiliar. The master at once recognized it as Ben Dabney, otherwise known as "Uncle Ben," a good-humored but not over-bright miner, who occupied a small cabin on an unambitious claim in the outskirts of Indian Spring. His avuncular title was evidently only an ironical tribute to his amiable incompetency and heavy good-nature, for he was still a young man with no family ties, and by reason of his singular shyness not even a visitor in the few families of the neighborhood. As the master looked up, he had an irritating recollection that Ben had been already haunting him for the last two days, alternately appearing and disappearing in his path to and from school as a more than usually reserved and bashful ghost. This, to the master's cynical mind, clearly indicated that, like most ghosts, he had something of essentially selfish import to communicate. Catching the apparition's half-appealing eye, he proceeded to exorcise it with a portentous frown and shake of the head, that caused it to timidly wane and fall away from the porch, only however to reappear and wax larger a few minutes later at one of the side windows. The infant class hailing his appearance as a heaven-sent boon, the master was obliged to walk to the door and command him sternly away, when, retreating to the fence, he mounted the uppermost rail, and drawing a knife from his pocket, cut a long splinter from the rail, and began to whittle it in patient and meditative silence. But when recess was declared, and the relieved feelings of the little flock had vent in the clearing around the schoolhouse, the few who rushed to the spot found that Uncle Ben had already disappeared. Whether the appearance of the children was too inconsistent with his ghostly mission, or whether his heart failed him at the last moment, the master could not determine. Yet, distasteful as the impending interview promised to be, the master was vaguely and irritatingly disappointed.

A few hours later, when school was being dismissed, the master found Octavia Dean lingering near his desk. Looking into the girl's mischievous eyes, he good-humoredly answered their expectation by referring to her morning's news. "I thought Miss McKinstry had been married by this time," he said carelessly.

Octavia, swinging her satchel like a censer, as if she were

performing some act of thurification over her completed tasks, replied demurely: "Oh no! dear no—not THAT."

"So it would seem," said the master.

"I reckon she never kalkilated to, either," continued Octavia, slyly looking up from the corner of her lashes.

"Indeed!"

"No—she was just funning with Seth Davis—that's all."

"Funning with him?"

"Yes, sir. Kinder foolin' him, you know."

"Kinder foolin' him!"

For an instant the master felt it his professional duty to protest against this most unmaidenly and frivolous treatment of the matrimonial engagement, but a second glance at the significant face of his youthful auditor made him conclude that her instinctive knowledge of her own sex could be better trusted than his imperfect theories. He turned towards his desk without speaking. Octavia gave an extra swing to her satchel, tossing it over her shoulder with a certain small coquettishness and moved towards the door. As she did so the infant Filgee from the safe vantage of the porch where he had lingered was suddenly impelled to a crowning audacity! As if struck with an original idea, but apparently addressing himself to space, he cried out, "Crethy M'Kinthry likth teacher," and instantly vanished.

Putting these incidents sternly aside, the master addressed himself to the task of setting a few copies for the next day as the voices of his departing flock faded from the porch.

Presently a silence fell upon the little school-house. Through the open door a cool, restful breath stole gently as if nature were again stealthily taking possession of her own. A squirrel boldly came across the porch, a few twittering birds charging in stopped, beat the air hesitatingly for a moment with their wings, and fell back with bashfully protesting breasts aslant against the open door and the unlooked-for spectacle of the silent occupant. Then there was another movement of intrusion, but this time human, and the master looked up angrily to behold Uncle Ben.

He entered with a slow exasperating step, lifting his large boots very high and putting them down again softly as if he were afraid of some insecurity in the floor, or figuratively recognized the fact that the pathways of knowledge were thorny and difficult. Reaching the master's desk and the ministering presence above it, he stopped awkwardly, and with the rim of his soft felt hat endeavored to wipe from his face the meek smile it had worn when he entered. It chanced also that he had halted before the minute stool of the infant Filgee, and his large figure instantly assumed such Brobdingnagian proportions in contrast that he became more embarrassed than ever. The master made no attempt to relieve him, but regarded him with cold interrogation.

"I reckoned," he began, leaning one hand on the master's desk with affected ease, as he dusted his leg with his hat with the other, "I reckoned—that is—I allowed—I orter say—that I'd find ye alone at this time. Ye gin'rally are, ye know. It's a nice, soothin', restful, stoodious time, when a man kin, so to speak, run back on his eddication and think of all he ever knowed. Ye're jist like me, and ye see I sorter spotted your ways to onct."

"Then why did you come here this morning and disturb the school?" demanded the master sharply.

"That's so, I sorter slipped up thar, didn't I?" said Uncle Ben with a smile of rueful assent. "You see I didn't allow to COME IN then, but on'y to hang round a leetle and kinder get used to it, and it to me."

"Used to what?" said the master impatiently, albeit with a slight softening at his intruder's penitent expression.

Uncle Ben did not reply immediately, but looked around as if for a seat, tried one or two benches and a desk with his large hand as if testing their security, and finally abandoning the idea as dangerous, seated himself on the raised platform beside the master's chair, having previously dusted it with the flap of his hat. Finding, however, that the attitude was not conducive to explanation, he presently rose again, and picking up one of the school-books from the master's desk eyed it unskilfully upside down, and then said hesitatingly,—

"I reckon ye ain't usin' Dobell's 'Rithmetic here?"

"No," said the master.

"That's bad. 'Pears to be played out—that Dobell feller. I was brought up on Dobell. And Parsings' Grammar? Ye don't seem to be a using Parsings' Grammar either?"

"No," said the master, relenting still more as he glanced at Uncle Ben's perplexed face with a faint smile.

"And I reckon you'd be saying the same of Jones' 'Stronomy and Algebry? Things hev changed. You've got all the new style here," he continued, with affected carelessness, but studiously avoiding the master's eye. "For a man ez wos brought up on Parsings, Dobell, and Jones, thar don't appear to be much show nowadays."

The master did not reply. Observing several shades of color chase each other on Uncle Ben's face, he bent his own gravely over his books. The act appeared to relieve his companion, who with his eyes still turned towards the window went on:

"Ef you'd had them books—which you haven't—I had it in my mind to ask you suthen'. I had an idea of—of—sort of reviewing my eddication. Kinder going over the old books agin—jist to pass the time. Sorter running in yer arter school hours and doin' a little practisin', eh? You looking on me as an extry scholar—and I payin' ye as sich—but keepin' it 'twixt ourselves, you know—just for a pastime, eh?"

As the master smilingly raised his head, he became suddenly and ostentatiously attracted to the window.

"Them jay birds out there is mighty peart, coming right up to the school-house! I reckon they think it sort o' restful too."

"But if you really mean it, couldn't you use these books, Uncle Ben?" said the master cheerfully. "I dare say there's little difference—the principle is the same, you know."

Uncle Ben's face, which had suddenly brightened, as suddenly fell. He took the book from the master's hand without meeting his eyes, held it at arm's length, turned it over and then laid it softly down upon the desk as if it were some excessively fragile article. "Certingly," he murmured, with assumed reflective ease. "Certingly. The principle's all there." Nevertheless he was quite breathless and a few beads of perspiration stood out upon his smooth, blank forehead.

"And as to writing, for instance," continued the master with increasing heartiness as he took notice of these phenomena, "you know ANY copy-book will do."

He handed his pen carelessly to Uncle Ben. The large hand that took it timidly not only trembled but grasped it with such fatal and hopeless unfamiliarity that the master was fain to walk to the window and observe the birds also.

"They're mighty bold—them jays," said Uncle Ben, laying down the pen with scrupulous exactitude beside the book and gazing at his fingers as if he had achieved a miracle of delicate manipulation. "They don't seem to be afeared of nothing, do they?"

There was another pause. The master suddenly turned from the window. "I tell you what, Uncle Ben," he said with prompt decision and unshaken gravity, "the only thing for you to do is to just throw over Dobell and Parsons and Jones and the old quill pen that I see you're accustomed to, and start in fresh as if you'd never known them. Forget 'em all, you know. It will be mighty hard of course to do that," he continued, looking out of the window, "but you must do it."

He turned back, the brightness that transfigured Uncle Ben's face at that moment brought a slight moisture into his own eyes. The humble seeker of knowledge said hurriedly that he would try.

"And begin again at the beginning," continued the master cheerfully. "Exactly like one of those—in fact, as if you REALLY were a child again."

"That's so," said Uncle Ben, rubbing his hands delightedly, "that's me! Why, that's jest what I was sayin' to Roop"—

"Then you've already been talking about it?" intercepted the master in some surprise. "I thought you wanted it kept secret?"

"Well, yes," responded Uncle Ben dubiously. "But you see I sorter agreed with Roop Filgee that if you took to my ideas and didn't object, I'd give him two bits* every time he'd kem here and help me of an arternoon when you was away and kinder stand guard around the school-house, you know, so as to keep the fellows off. And Roop's mighty sharp for a boy, ye know."

    * Two bits, i. e., twenty-five cents.

The master reflected a moment and concluded that Uncle Ben was probably right. Rupert Filgee, who was a handsome boy of fourteen, was also a strongly original character whose youthful cynicism and blunt, honest temper had always attracted him. He was a fair scholar, with a possibility of being a better one, and the proposed arrangement with Uncle Ben would not interfere with the discipline of school hours and might help them both. Nevertheless he asked good-humoredly, "But couldn't you do this more securely and easily in your own house? I might lend you the books, you know, and come to you twice a week."

Uncle Ben's radiant face suddenly clouded. "It wouldn't be exactly the same kind o' game to me an' Roop," he said hesitatingly. "You see thar's the idea o' the school-house, ye know, and the restfulness and the quiet, and the gen'ral air o' study. And the boys around town ez wouldn't think nothin' o' trapsen' into my cabin if they spotted what I was up to thar, would never dream o' hunting me here."

"Very well," said the master, "let it be here then." Observing that his companion seemed to be struggling with an inarticulate gratitude and an apparently inextricable buckskin purse in his pocket, he added quietly, "I'll set you a few copies to commence with," and began to lay out a few unfinished examples of Master Johnny Filgee's scholastic achievements.

"After thanking YOU, Mr. Ford," said Uncle Ben, faintly, "ef you'll jest kinder signify, you know, what you consider a fair"—

Mr. Ford turned quickly and dexterously offered his hand to his companion in such a manner that he was obliged to withdraw his own from his pocket to grasp it in return. "You're very welcome," said the master, "and as I can only permit this sort of thing gratuitously, you'd better NOT let me know that you propose giving anything even to Rupert." He shook Uncle Ben's perplexed hand again, briefly explained what he had to do, and saying that he would now leave him alone a few minutes, he took his hat and walked towards the door.

"Then you reckon," said Uncle Ben slowly, regarding the work before him, "that I'd better jest chuck them Dobell fellers overboard?"

"I certainly should," responded the master with infinite gravity.

"And sorter waltz in fresh, like one them children?"

"Like a child," nodded the master as he left the porch.

A few moments later, as he was finishing his cigar in the clearing, he paused to glance in at the school-room window. Uncle Ben, stripped of his coat and waistcoat, with his shirt-sleeves rolled up on his powerful arms, had evidently cast Dobell and all misleading extraneous aid aside, and with the perspiration standing out on his foolish forehead, and his perplexed face close to the master's desk, was painfully groping along towards the light in the tottering and devious tracks of Master Johnny Filgee, like a very child indeed!

CHAPTER II

As the children were slowly straggling to their places the next morning, the master waited for an opportunity to speak to Rupert. That beautiful but scarcely amiable youth was, as usual, surrounded and impeded by a group of his small female admirers, for whom, it is but just to add, he had a supreme contempt. Possibly it was this healthy quality that inclined the master towards him, and it was consequently with some satisfaction that he overheard fragments of his openly disparaging comments upon his worshippers.

"There!" to Clarinda Jones, "don't flop! And don't YOU," to Octavia Dean, "go on breathing over my head like that. If there's anything I hate it's having a girl breathing round me. Yes, you were! I felt it in my hair. And YOU too—you're always snoopin' and snoodgin'. Oh, yes, you want to know WHY I've got an extry copy-book and another 'Rithmetic, Miss Curiosity. Well, what would you give to know? Want to see if they're PRETTY" (with infinite scorn at the adjective). "No, they ain't PRETTY. That's all you girls think about—what's PRETTY and what's curious! Quit now! Come! Don't ye see teacher lookin' at you? Ain't you ashamed?"

He caught the master's beckoning eye and came forward, slightly abashed, with a flush of irritation still on his handsome face, and his chestnut curls slightly rumpled. One, which Octavia had covertly accented by twisting round her forefinger, stood up like a crest on his head.

"I've told Uncle Ben that you might help him here after school hours," said the master, taking him aside. "You may therefore omit your writing exercise in the morning and do it in the afternoon."

The boy's dark eyes sparkled. "And if it would be all the same to you, sir," he added earnestly, "you might sorter give out in school that I was to be kept in."

"I'm afraid that would hardly do," said the master, much amused. "But why?"

Rupert's color deepened. "So ez to keep them darned girls from foolin' round me and followin' me back here."

"We will attend to that," said the master smiling; a moment after he added more seriously, "I suppose your father knows that you are to receive money for this? And he doesn't object?"

"He! Oh no!" returned Rupert with a slight look of astonishment, and the same general suggestion of patronizing his progenitor that he had previously shown to his younger brother. "You needn't mind HIM." In reality Filgee pere, a widower of two years' standing, had tacitly allowed the discipline of his family to devolve upon Rupert. Remembering this, the master could only say, "Very well," and good-naturedly dismiss the pupil to his seat and the subject from his mind. The last laggard had just slipped in, the master had glanced over the occupied benches with his hand upon his warning bell, when there was a quick step on the gravel, a flutter of skirts like the sound of alighting birds, and a young woman lightly entered.

In the rounded, untouched, and untroubled freshness of her cheek and chin, and the forward droop of her slender neck, she appeared a girl of fifteen; in her developed figure and the maturer drapery of her full skirts she seemed a woman; in her combination of naive recklessness and perfect understanding of her person she was both. In spite of a few school-books that jauntily swung from a strap in her gloved hand, she bore no resemblance to a pupil; in her pretty gown of dotted muslin with bows of blue ribbon on the skirt and corsage, and a cluster of roses in her belt, she was as inconsistent and incongruous to the others as a fashion-plate would have been in the dry and dog-eared pages before them. Yet she carried it off with a demure mingling of the naivete of youth and the aplomb of a woman, and as she swept down the narrow aisle, burying a few small wondering heads in the overflow of her flounces, there was no doubt of her reception in the arch smile that dimpled her cheek. Dropping a half curtsey to the master, the only suggestion of her equality with the others, she took her place at one of the larger desks, and resting her elbow on the lid began to quietly remove her gloves. It was Cressy McKinstry.

Irritated and disturbed at the girl's unceremonious entrance, the master for the moment recognized her salutation coldly, and affected to ignore her elaborate appearance. The situation was embarrassing. He could not decline to receive her as she was no longer accompanied by her lover, nor could he plead entire ignorance of her broken engagement; while to point out the glaring inappropriateness of costume would be a fresh interference he knew Indian Spring would scarcely tolerate. He could only accept such explanation as she might choose to give. He rang his bell as much to avert the directed eyes of the children as to bring the scene to a climax.

She had removed her gloves and was standing up.

"I reckon I can go on where I left off?" she said lazily, pointing to the books she had brought with her.

"For the present," said the master dryly.

The first class was called. Later, when his duty brought him to her side, he was surprised to find that she was evidently already prepared with consecutive lessons, as if she were serenely unconscious of any doubt of her return, and as coolly as if she had only left school the day before. Her studies were still quite elementary, for Cressy McKinstry had never been a brilliant scholar, but he perceived, with a cynical doubt of its permanency, that she had bestowed unusual care upon her present performance. There was moreover a certain defiance in it, as if she had resolved to stop any objection to her return on the score of deficiencies. He was obliged in self-defence to take particular note of some rings she wore, and a large bracelet that ostentatiously glittered on her white arm—which had already attracted the attention of her companions, and prompted the audible comment from Johnny Filgee that it was "truly gold." Without meeting her eyes he contented himself with severely restraining the glances of the children that wandered in her direction. She had never been quite popular with the school in her previous role of fiancée, and only Octavia Dean and one or two older girls appreciated its mysterious fascination; while the beautiful Rupert, secure in his avowed predilection for the middle-aged wife of the proprietor of the Indian Spring hotel, looked upon her as a precocious chit with more than the usual propensity to objectionable "breathing." Nevertheless the master was irritatingly conscious of her presence—a presence which now had all the absurdity of her ridiculous love-experiences superadded to it. He tried to reason with himself that it was only a phase of frontier life, which ought to have amused him. But it did not. The intrusion of this preposterous girl seemed to disarrange the discipline of his life as well as of his school. The usual vague, far-off dreams in which he was in the habit of indulging during school-hours, dreams that were perhaps superinduced by the remoteness of his retreat and a certain restful sympathy in his little auditors, which had made him— the grown-up dreamer—acceptable to them in his gentle understanding of their needs and weaknesses, now seemed to have vanished forever.

At recess, Octavia Dean, who had drawn near Cressy and reached up to place her arm round the older girl's waist, glanced at her with a patronizing smile born of some rapid free-masonry, and laughingly retired with the others. The master at his desk, and Cressy who had halted in the aisle were left alone.

"I have had no intimation yet from your father or mother that you were coming back to school again," he began. "But I suppose THEY have decided upon your return?"

An uneasy suspicion of some arrangement with her former lover had prompted the emphasis.

The young girl looked at him with languid astonishment. "I reckon paw and maw ain't no objection," she said with the same easy ignoring of parental authority that had charac- terized Rupert Filgee, and which seemed to be a local peculiarity. "Maw DID offer to come yer and see you, but I told her she needn't bother."

She rested her two hands behind her on the edge of a desk, and leaned against it, looking down upon the toe of her smart little shoe which was describing a small semicircle beyond the hem of her gown. Her attitude, which was half-defiant, half-indolent, brought out the pretty curves of her waist and shoulders. The master noticed it and became a trifle more austere.

"Then I am to understand that this is a permanent thing?" he asked coldly.

"What's that?" said Cressy interrogatively.

"Am I to understand that you intend coming regularly to school?" repeated the master curtly, "or is this merely an arrangement for a few days—until"—

"Oh," said Cressy comprehendingly, lifting her unabashed blue eyes to his, "you mean THAT. Oh, THAT'S broke off. Yes," she added contemptuously, making a larger semicircle with her foot, "that's over—three weeks ago."

"And Seth Davis—does HE intend returning too?"

"He!" She broke into a light girlish laugh. "I reckon not much! S'long's I'm here, at least." She had just lifted herself to a sitting posture on the desk, so that her little feet swung clear of the floor in their saucy dance. Suddenly she brought her heels together and alighted. "So that's all?" she asked.

"Yes."

"Kin I go now?"

"Yes."

She laid her books one on the top of the other and lingered an instant.

"Been quite well?" she asked with indolent politeness.

"Yes—thank you."

"You're lookin' right peart."

She walked with a Southern girl's undulating languor to the door, opened it, then charged suddenly upon Octavia Dean, twirled her round in a wild waltz and bore her away; appearing a moment after on the playground demurely walking with her arm around her companion's waist in an ostentatious confidence at once lofty, exclusive, and exasperating to the smaller children.

When school was dismissed that afternoon and the master had remained to show Rupert Filgee how to prepare Uncle Ben's tasks, and had given his final instructions to his youthful vicegerent, that irascible Adonis unburdened himself querulously:

"Is Cressy McKinstry comin' reg'lar, Mr. Ford?"

"She is," said the master dryly. After a pause he asked, "Why?"

Rupert's curls had descended on his eyebrows in heavy discontent. "It's mighty rough, jest ez a feller reckons he's got quit of her and her jackass bo', to hev her prancin' back inter school agin, and rigged out like ez if she'd been to a fire in a milliner's shop."

"You shouldn't allow your personal dislikes, Rupert, to provoke you to speak of a fellow-scholar in that way—and a young lady, too," corrected the master dryly.

"The woods is full o' sich feller-scholars and sich young ladies, if yer keer to go a gunning for 'em," said Rupert with dark and slangy significance. "Ef I'd known she was comin' back I'd"—he stopped and brought his sunburnt fist against the seam of his trousers with a boyish gesture, "I'd hev jist"—

"What?" said the master sharply.

"I'd hev played hookey till she left school agin! It moutn't hev bin so long, neither," he added with a mysterious chuckle.

"That will do," said the master peremptorily. "For the present you'll attend to your duty and try to make Uncle Ben see you're something more than a foolish, prejudiced school-boy, or," he added significantly, "he and I may both repent our agreement. Let me have a good account of you both when I return."

He took his hat from its peg on the wall, and in obedience to a suddenly formed resolution left the school-room to call upon the parents of Cressy McKinstry. He was not quite certain what he should say, but, after his habit, would trust to the inspiration of the moment. At the worst he could resign a situation that now appeared to require more tact and delicacy than seemed consistent with his position, and he was obliged to confess to himself that he had lately suspected that his present occupation—the temporary expedient of a poor but clever young man of twenty—was scarcely bringing him nearer a realization of his daily dreams. For Mr. Jack Ford was a youthful pilgrim who had sought his fortune in California so lightly equipped that even in the matter of kin and advisers he was deficient. That prospective fortune had already eluded him in San Francisco, had apparently not waited for him in Sacramento, and now seemed never to have been at Indian Spring. Nevertheless, when he was once out of sight of the school-house he lit a cigar, put his hands in his pockets, and strode on with the cheerfulness of that youth to which all things are possible.

The children had already dispersed as mysteriously and completely as they had arrived. Between him and the straggling hamlet of Indian Spring the landscape seemed to be without sound or motion. The wooded upland or ridge on which the schoolhouse stood, half a mile further on, began to slope gradually towards the river, on whose banks, seen from that distance, the town appeared to have been scattered irregularly or thrown together hastily, as if cast ashore by some overflow—the Cosmopolitan Hotel drifting into the Baptist church, and dragging in its tail of wreckage two saloons and a blacksmith's shop; while the County Courthouse was stranded in solitary grandeur in a waste of gravel half a mile away. The intervening flat was still gashed and furrowed by the remorseless engines of earlier gold-seekers.

Mr. Ford was in little sympathy with this unsuccessful record of frontier endeavor—the fortune HE had sought did not seem to lie in that direction—and his eye glanced quickly beyond it to the pine-crested hills across the river, whose primeval security was so near and yet so inviolable, or back again to the trail he was pursuing along the ridge. The latter prospect still retained its semi-savage character in spite of the occasional suburban cottages of residents, and the few outlying farms or ranches of the locality. The grounds of the cottages were yet uncleared of underbrush; bear and catamount still prowled around the rude fences of the ranches; the late alleged experience of the infant Snyder was by no means improbable or unprecedented.

A light breeze was seeking the heated flat and river, and thrilling the leaves around him with the strong vitality of the forest. The vibrating cross-lights and tremulous chequers of shade cast by the stirred foliage seemed to weave a fantastic net around him as he walked. The quaint odors of certain woodland herbs known to his scholars, and religiously kept in their desks, or left like votive offerings on the threshold of the school-house, recalled all the primitive simplicity and delicious wildness of the little temple he had left. Even in the mischievous glances of evasive squirrels and the moist eyes of the contemplative rabbits there were faint suggestions of some of his own truants. The woods were trembling with gentle memories of the independence he had always known here—of that sweet and grave retreat now so ridiculously invaded.

He began to hesitate, with one of those revulsions of sentiment characteristic of his nature: Why should he bother himself about this girl after all? Why not make up his mind to accept her as his predecessor had done? Why was it necessary for him to find her inconsistent with his ideas of duty to his little flock and his mission to them? Was he not assuming a sense of decorum that was open to misconception? The absurdity of her school costume, and any responsibility it incurred, rested not with him but with her parents. What right had he to point it out to them, and above all how was he to do it? He halted irresolutely at what he believed was his sober second thought, but which, like most reflections that take that flattering title, was only a reaction as impulsive and illogical as the emotion that preceded it.

Mr. McKinstry's "snake rail" fence was already discernible in the lighter opening of the woods, not far from where he had halted. As he stood there in hesitation, the pretty figure and bright gown of Cressy McKinstry suddenly emerged from a more secluded trail that intersected his own at an acute angle a few rods ahead of him. She was not alone, but was accompanied by a male figure whose arm she had evidently just dislodged from her waist. He was still trying to resume his lost vantage; she was as resolutely evading him with a certain nymph-like agility, while the sound of her half-laughing, half-irate protest could be faintly heard. Without being able to identify the face or figure of her companion at that distance, he could see that it was NOT her former betrothed, Seth Davis.

A superior smile crossed his face; he no longer hesitated, but at once resumed his former path. For some time Cressy and her companion moved on quietly before him. Then on reaching the rail-fence they turned abruptly to the right, were lost for an instant in the intervening thicket, and the next moment Cressy appeared alone, crossing the meadow in a shorter cut towards the house, having either scaled the fence or slipped through some familiar gap. Her companion had disappeared. Whether they had noticed that they were observed he could not determine. He kept steadily along the trail that followed the line of fence to the lane that led directly to the farm-building, and pushed open the front gate as Cressy's light dress vanished round an angle at the rear of the house.

The house of the McKinstrys rose, or rather stretched, itself before him, in all the lazy ungainliness of Southwestern architecture. A collection of temporary make-shifts of boards, of logs, of canvas, prematurely decayed, and in some instances abandoned for a newer erection, or degraded to mere outhouses—it presented with singular frankness the nomadic and tentative disposition of its founder. It had been repaired without being improved; its additions had seemed only to extend its primitive ugliness over a larger space. Its roofs were roughly shingled or rudely boarded and battened, and the rafters of some of its "lean-to's" were simply covered with tarred canvas. As if to settle any doubt of the impossibility of this heterogeneous mass ever taking upon itself any picturesque combination, a small building of corrugated iron, transported in sections from some remoter locality, had been set up in its centre. The McKinstry ranch had long been an eyesore to the master: even that morning he had been mutely wondering from what convolution of that hideous chrysalis the bright butterfly Cressy had emerged. It was with a renewal of this curiosity that he had just seen her flutter back to it again.

A yellow dog who had observed him hesitating in doubt where he should enter, here yawned, rose from the sunlight where he had been blinking, approached the master with languid politeness, and then turned towards the iron building as if showing him the way. Mr. Ford followed him cautiously, painfully conscious that his hypocritical canine introducer was only availing himself of an opportunity to gain ingress into the house, and was leading him as a responsible accomplice to probable exposure and disgrace. His expectation was quickly realized: a lazily querulous, feminine outcry, with the words, "Yer's that darned hound agin!" came from an adjacent room, and his exposed and abashed companion swiftly retreated past him into the road again. Mr. Ford found himself alone in a plainly-furnished sitting-room confronting the open door leading to another apartment at which the figure of a woman, preceded hastily by a thrown dishcloth, had just appeared. It was Mrs. McKinstry; her sleeves were rolled up over her red but still shapely arms, and as she stood there wiping them on her apron, with her elbows advanced, and her closed hands raised alternately in the air, there was an odd pugilistic suggestion in her attitude. It was not lessened on her sudden discovery of the master by her retreating backwards with her hands up and her elbows still well forward as if warily retiring to an imaginary "corner."

Mr. Ford at once tactfully stepped back from the doorway. "I beg your pardon," he said, delicately addressing the opposite wall, "but I found the door open and I followed the dog."

"That's just one of his pizenous tricks," responded Mrs. McKinstry dolefully from within. "On'y last week he let in a Chinaman, and in the nat'ral hustlin' that follered he managed to help himself outer the pork bar'l. There ain't no shade o' cussedness that or'nary hound ain't up to." Yet notwithstanding this ominous comparison she presently made her appearance with her sleeves turned down, her black woollen dress "tidied," and a smile of fatigued but not unkindly welcome and protection on her face. Dusting a chair with her apron and placing it before the master, she continued maternally, "Now that you're here, set ye right down and make yourself to home. My men folks are all out o' door, but some of 'em's sure to happen in soon for suthin'; that day ain't yet created that they don't come huntin' up Mammy McKinstry every five minutes for this thing or that."

The glow of a certain hard pride burned through the careworn languor of her brown cheek. What she had said was strangely true. This raw-boned woman before him, although scarcely middle-aged, had for years occupied a self-imposed maternal and protecting relation, not only to her husband and brothers, but to the three or four men, who as partners, or hired hands, lived at the ranch. An inherited and trained sympathy with what she called her "boys's" and her "men folk," and their needs had partly unsexed her. She was a fair type of a class not uncommon on the Southwestern frontier; women who were ruder helpmeets of their rude husbands and brothers, who had shared their privations and sufferings with surly, masculine endurance, rather than feminine patience; women who had sent their loved ones to hopeless adventure or terrible vendetta as a matter of course, or with partisan fury; who had devotedly nursed the wounded to keep alive the feud, or had received back their dead dry-eyed and revengeful. Small wonder that Cressy McKinstry had developed strangely under this sexless relationship. Looking at the mother, albeit not without a certain respect, Mr. Ford found himself contrasting her with the daughter's graceful femininity, and wondering where in Cressy's youthful contour the possibility of the grim figure before him was even now hidden.

"Hiram allowed to go over to the schoolhouse and see you this mornin'," said Mrs. McKinstry, after a pause; "but I reckon ez how he had to look up stock on the river. The cattle are that wild this time o' year, huntin' water, and hangin' round the tules, that my men are nigh worrited out o' their butes with 'em. Hank and Jim ain't been off their mustangs since sun up, and Hiram, what with partrollen' the West Boundary all night, watchin' stakes whar them low down Harrisons hev been trespassin'—hasn't put his feet to the ground in fourteen hours. Mebbee you noticed Hiram ez you kem along? Ef so, ye didn't remember what kind o' shootin' irons he had with him? I see his rifle over yon. Like ez not he'z only got his six-shooter, and them Harrisons are mean enough to lay for him at long range. But," she added, returning to the less important topic, "I s'pose Cressy came all right."

"Yes," said the master hopelessly.

"I reckon she looked so," continued Mrs. McKinstry, with tolerant abstraction. "She allowed to do herself credit in one of them new store gownds that she got at Sacramento. At least that's what some of our men said. Late years, I ain't kept tech with the fashions myself." She passed her fingers explanatorily down the folds of her own coarse gown, but without regret or apology.

"She seemed well prepared in her lessons," said the master, abandoning for the moment that criticism of his pupil's dress, which he saw was utterly futile, "but am I to understand that she is coming regularly to school—that she is now perfectly free to give her entire attention to her studies—that—that—her—engagement is broken off?"

"Why, didn't she tell ye?" echoed Mrs. McKinstry in languid surprise.

"SHE certainly did," said the master with slight embarrassment, "but"—

"Ef SHE said so," interrupted Mrs. McKinstry abstractedly, "she oughter know, and you kin tie to what she says."

"But as I'm responsible to PARENTS and not to scholars for the discipline of my school," returned the young man a little stiffly, "I thought it my duty to hear it from YOU."

"That's so," said Mrs. McKinstry meditatively; "then I reckon you'd better see Hiram. That ar' Seth Davis engagement was a matter of hern and her father's, and not in MY line. I 'spose that Hiram nat'rally allows to set the thing square to you and inquirin' friends."

"I hope you understand," said the master, slightly resenting the classification, "that my reason for inquiring about the permanency of your daughter's attendance was simply because it might be necessary to arrange her studies in a way more suitable to her years; perhaps even to suggest to you that a young ladies' seminary might be more satisfactory"—

"Sartain, sartain," interrupted Mrs. McKinstry hurriedly, but whether from evasion of annoying suggestion or weariness of the topic, the master could not determine. "You'd better speak to Hiram about it. On'y," she hesitated slightly, "ez he's got now sorter set and pinted towards your school, and is a trifle worrited with stock and them Harrisons, ye might tech it lightly. He oughter be along yer now. I can't think what keeps him." Her eye wandered again with troubled preoccupation to the corner where her husband's Sharps' rifle stood. Suddenly she raised her voice as if forgetful of Mr. Ford's presence.

"O Cressy!"

"O Maw!"

The response came from the inner room. The next moment Cressy appeared at the door with an odd half-lazy defiance in her manner, which the master could not understand except upon the hypothesis that she had been listening. She had already changed her elaborate toilet for a long clinging, coarse blue gown, that accented the graceful curves of her slight, petticoat-less figure. Nodding her head towards the master, she said, "Howdy?" and turned to her mother, who practically ignored their personal acquaintance. "Cressy," she said, "Dad's gone and left his Sharps' yer, d'ye mind takin' it along to meet him, afore he passes the Boundary corner. Ye might tell him the teacher's yer, wantin' to see him."

"One moment," said the master, as the young girl carelessly stepped to the corner and lifted the weapon. "Let ME take it. It's all on my way back to school and I'll meet him."

Mrs. McKinstry looked perturbed. Cressy opened her clear eyes on the master with evident surprise. "No, Mr. Ford," said Mrs. McKinstry, with her former maternal manner. "Ye'd better not mix yourself up with these yer doin's. Ye've no call to do it, and Cressy has; it's all in the family. But it's outer YOUR line, and them Harrison whelps go to your school. Fancy the teacher takin' weppins betwixt and between!"

"It's fitter work for the teacher than for one of his scholars, and a young lady at that," said Mr. Ford gravely, as he took the rifle from the hands of the half-amused, half-reluctant girl. "It's quite safe with me, and I promise I shall deliver it into Mr. McKinstry's hands and none other."

"Perhaps it wouldn't be ez likely to be gin'rally noticed ez it would if one of US carried it," murmured Mrs. McKinstry in confidential abstraction, gazing at her daughter sublimely unconscious of the presence of a third party.

"You're quite right," said the master composedly, throwing the rifle over his shoulder and turning towards the door. "So I'll say good-afternoon, and try and find your husband."

Mrs. McKinstry constrainedly plucked at the folds of her coarse gown. "Ye'll like a drink afore ye go," she said, in an ill-concealed tone of relief. "I clean forgot my manners. Cressy, fetch out that demijohn."

"Not for me, thank you," returned Mr. Ford smiling.

"Oh, I see—you're temperance, nat'rally," said Mrs. McKinstry with a tolerant sigh.

"Hardly that," returned the master, "I follow no rule, I drink sometimes—but not to-day."

Mrs. McKinstry's dark face contracted. "Don't you see, Maw," struck in Cressy quickly. "Teacher drinks sometimes, but he don't USE whiskey. That's all."

Her mother's face relaxed. Cressy slipped out of the door before the master, and preceded him to the gate. When she had reached it she turned and looked into his face.

"What did Maw say to yer about seein' me just now?"

"I don't understand you."

"To your seein' me and Joe Masters on the trail?"

"She said nothing."

"Humph," said Cressy meditatively. "What was it you told her about it?"

"Nothing."

"Then you DIDN'T see us?"

"I saw you with some one—I don't know whom."

"And you didn't tell Maw?"

"I did not. It was none of my business."

He instantly saw the utter inconsistency of this speech in connection with the reason he believed he had in coming. But it was too late to recall it, and she was looking at him with a bright but singular expression.

"That Joe Masters is the conceitedest fellow goin'. I told him you could see his foolishness."

"Ah, indeed."

Mr. Ford pushed open the gate. As the girl still lingered he was obliged to hold it a moment before passing through.

"Maw couldn't quite hitch on to your not drinkin'. She reckons you're like everybody else about yer. That's where she slips up on you. And everybody else, I kalkilate."

"I suppose she's somewhat anxious about your father, and I dare say is expecting me to hurry," returned the master pointedly.

"Oh, dad's all right," said Cressy mischievously. "You'll come across him over yon, in the clearing. But you're looking right purty with that gun. It kinder sets you off. You oughter wear one."

The master smiled slightly, said "Good-by," and took leave of the girl, but not of her eyes, which were still following him. Even when he had reached the end of the lane and glanced back at the rambling dwelling, she was still leaning on the gate with one foot on the lower rail and her chin cupped in the hollow of her hand. She made a slight gesture, not clearly intelligible at that distance; it might have been a mischievous imitation of the way he had thrown the gun over his shoulder, it might have been a wafted kiss.

The master however continued his way in no very self-satisfied mood. Although he did not regret having taken the place of Cressy as the purveyor of lethal weapons between the belligerent parties, he knew he was tacitly mingling in the feud between people for whom he cared little or nothing. It was true that the Harrisons sent their children to his school, and that in the fierce partisanship of the locality this simple courtesy was open to misconstruction. But he was more uneasily conscious that this mission, so far as Mrs. McKinstry was concerned, was a miserable failure. The strange relations of the mother and daughter perhaps explained much of the girl's conduct, but it offered no hope of future amelioration. Would the father, "worried by stock" and boundary quarrels—a man in the habit of cutting Gordian knots with a bowie knife—prove more reasonable? Was there any nearer sympathy between father and daughter? But she had said he would meet McKinstry in the clearing: she was right, for here he was coming forward at a gallop!

Bret Harte

CHAPTER III

When within a dozen paces of the master, McKinstry, scarcely checking his mustang, threw himself from the saddle, and with a sharp cut of his riata on the animal's haunches sent him still galloping towards the distant house. Then, with both hands deeply thrust in the side pockets of his long, loose linen coat, he slowly lounged with clanking spurs towards the young man. He was thick-set, of medium height, densely and reddishly bearded, with heavy-lidded pale blue eyes that wore a look of drowsy pain, and after their first wearied glance at the master, seemed to rest anywhere but on him.

"Your wife was sending you your rifle by Cressy," said the master, "but I offered to bring it myself, as I thought it scarcely a proper errand for a young lady. Here it is. I hope you didn't miss it before and don't require it now," he added quietly.

Mr. McKinstry took it in one hand with an air of slightly embarrassed surprise, rested it against his shoulder, and then with the same hand and without removing the other from his pocket, took off his soft felt hat, showed a bullet-hole in its rim, and returned lazily, "It's about half an hour late, but them Harrisons reckoned I was fixed for 'em and war too narvous to draw a clear bead on me."

The moment was evidently not a felicitous one for the master's purpose, but he was determined to go on. He hesitated an instant, when his companion, who seemed to be equally but more sluggishly embarrassed, in a moment of preoccupied perplexity withdrew from his pocket his right hand swathed in a blood-stained bandage, and following some instinctive habit, attempted, as if reflectively, to scratch his head with two stiffened fingers.

"You are hurt," said the master, genuinely shocked, "and here I am detaining you."

"I had my hand up—so," explained McKinstry, with heavy deliberation, "and the ball raked off my little finger after it went through my hat. But that ain't what I wanted to say when I stopped ye. I ain't just kam enough yet," he apologized in the calmest manner, "and I clean forgit myself," he added with perfect self-possession. "But I was kalkilatin' to ask you"—he laid his bandaged hand familiarly on the master's shoulder—"if Cressy kem all right?"

"Perfectly," said the master. "But shan't I walk on home with you, and we can talk together after your wound is attended to?"

"And she looked purty?" continued McKinstry without moving.

"Very."

"And you thought them new store gownds of hers right peart?"

"Yes," said the master. "Perhaps a little too fine for the school, you know," he added insinuatingly, "and"—

"Not for her—not for her," interrupted McKinstry. "I reckon thar's more whar that cam from! Ye needn't fear but that she kin keep up that gait ez long ez Hiram McKinstry hez the runnin' of her."

Mr. Ford gazed hopelessly at the hideous ranch in the distance, at the sky, and the trail before him; then his glance fell upon the hand still upon his shoulder, and he struggled with a final effort. "At another time I'd like to have a long talk with you about your daughter, Mr. McKinstry."

"Talk on," said McKinstry, putting his wounded hand through the master's arm. "I admire to hear you. You're that kam, it does me good."

Nevertheless the master was conscious that his own arm was scarcely as firm as his companion's. It was however useless to draw back now, and with as much tact as he could command he relieved his mind of its purpose. Addressing the obtruding bandage before him, he dwelt upon Cressy's previous attitude in the school, the danger of any relapse, the necessity of her having a more clearly defined position as a scholar, and even the advisability of her being transferred to a more advanced school with a more mature teacher of her own sex. "This is what I wished to say to Mrs. McKinstry to-day," he concluded, "but she referred me to you."

"In course, in course," said McKinstry, nodding compla-cently. "She's a good woman in and around the ranch, and in any doin's o' this kind," he lightly waved his wounded arm in the air, "there ain't a better, tho' I say it. She was Blair Rawlins' darter; she and her brother Clay bein' the only ones that kem out safe arter their twenty years' fight with the McEntees in West Kaintuck. But she don't understand gals ez you and me do. Not that I'm much, ez I orter be more kam. And the old woman jest sized the hull thing when she said SHE hadn't any hand in Cressy's engagement. No more she had! And ez far ez that goes, no more did me, nor Seth Davis, nor Cressy." He paused, and lifting his heavy-lidded eyes to the master for the second time, said reflectively, "Ye mustn't mind my tellin' ye—ez betwixt man and man—that THE one ez is most responsible for the makin' and breakin' o' that engagement is YOU!"

"Me!" said the master in utter bewilderment.

"You!" repeated McKinstry quietly, reinstalling the hand Ford had attempted to withdraw. "I ain't sayin' ye either know'd it or kalkilated on it. But it war so. Ef ye'd hark to me, and meander on a little, I'll tell ye HOW it war. I don't mind walkin' a piece YOUR way, for if we go towards the ranch, and the hounds see me, they'll set up a racket and bring out the old woman, and then good-by to any confidential talk betwixt you and me. And I'm, somehow, kammer out yer."

He moved slowly down the trail, still holding Ford's arm confidentially, although, owing to his large protecting manner, he seemed to offer a ridiculous suggestion of supporting HIM with his wounded member.

"When you first kem to Injin Spring," he began, "Seth and Cressy was goin' to school, boy and girl like, and nothin' more. They'd known each other from babies—the Davises bein' our neighbors in Kaintuck, and emigraten' with us from St. Joe. Seth mout hev cottoned to Cress, and Cress to him, in course o' time, and there wasn't anythin' betwixt the families to hev kept 'em from marryin' when they wanted. But there never war any words passed, and no engagement."

"But," interrupted Ford hastily, "my predecessor, Mr. Martin, distinctly told me that there was, and that it was with

YOUR permission."

"That's only because you noticed suthin' the first day you looked over the school with Martin. 'Dad,' sez Cress to me, 'that new teacher's very peart; and he's that keen about noticin' me and Seth that I reckon you'd better giv out that we're engaged.' 'But are you?' sez I. 'It'll come to that in the end,' sez Cress, 'and if that yer teacher hez come here with Northern ideas o' society, it's just ez well to let him see Injin Spring ain't entirely in the woods about them things either.' So I agreed, and Martin told you it was all right; Cress and Seth was an engaged couple, and you was to take no notice. And then YOU ups and objects to the hull thing, and allows that courtin' in school, even among engaged pupils, ain't proper."

The master turned his eyes with some uneasiness to the face of Cressy's father. It was heavy but impassive.

"I don't mind tellin' you, now that it's over, what happened. The trouble with me, Mr. Ford, is—I ain't kam! and YOU air, and that's what got me. For when I heard what you'd said, I got on that mustang and started for the school-house to clean you out and giv' you five minutes to leave Injin Spring. I don't know ez you remember that day. I'd kalkilated my time so ez to ketch ye comin' out o' school, but I was too airly. I hung around out o' sight, and then hitched my hoss to a buckeye and peeped inter the winder to hev a good look at ye. It was very quiet and kam. There was squirrels over the roof, yellow-jackets and bees dronin' away, and kinder sleeping-like all around in the air, and jay-birds twitterin' in the shingles, and they never minded me. You were movin' up and down among them little gals and boys, liftin' up their heads and talkin' to 'em softly and quiet like, ez if you was one of them yourself. And they looked contented and kam. And onct—I don't know if YOU remember it—you kem close up to the winder with your hands behind you, and looked out so kam and quiet and so far off, ez if everybody else outside the school was miles away from you. It kem to me then that I'd given a heap to hev had the old woman see you thar. It kem to me, Mr. Ford, that there wasn't any place for ME thar; and it kem to me, too—and a little rough like—that mebbe there wasn't any place there for MY Cress either! So I rode away without disturbin' you nor the birds nor the squirrels. Talkin' with Cress that night, she said ez how it was a fair sample of what happened every day, and that you'd always treated her fair like the others. So she allowed that she'd go down to Sacramento, and get some things agin her and Seth bein' married next month, and she reckoned she wouldn't trouble you nor the school agin. Hark till I've done, Mr. Ford," he continued, as the young man made a slight movement of deprecation. "Well, I agreed. But arter she got to Sacramento and bought some fancy fixin's, she wrote to me and sez ez how she'd been thinkin' the hull thing over, and she reckoned that she and Seth were too young to marry, and the engagement had better be broke. And I broke it for her."

"But how?" asked the bewildered master.

"Gin'rally with this gun," returned McKinstry with slow gravity, indicating the rifle he was carrying, "for I ain't kam. I let on to Seth's father that if I ever found Seth and Cressy together again, I'd shoot him. It made a sort o' coolness betwixt the families, and hez given some comfort to them low-down Harrisons; but even the law, I reckon, recognizes a father's rights. And ez Cress sez, now ez Seth's out o' the way, thar ain't no reason why she can't go back to school and finish her eddication. And I reckoned she was right. And we both agreed that ez she'd left school to git them store clothes, it was only fair that she'd give the school the benefit of 'em."

The case seemed more hopeless than ever. The master knew that the man beside him might hardly prove as lenient to a second objection at his hand. But that very reason, perhaps, impelled him, now that he knew his danger, to consider it more strongly as a duty, and his pride revolted from a possible threat underlying McKinstry's confidences. Nevertheless he began gently:

"But you are quite sure you won't regret that you didn't avail yourself of this broken engagement, and your daughter's outfit—to send her to some larger boarding-school in Sacramento or San Francisco? Don't you think she may find it dull, and soon tire of the company of mere children when she has already known the excitement of"—he was about to say "a lover," but checked himself, and added, "a young girl's freedom?"

"Mr. Ford," returned McKinstry, with the slow and fatuous misconception of a one-ideaed man, "when I said just now that, lookin' inter that kam, peaceful school of yours, I didn't find a place for Cress, it warn't because I didn't think she OUGHTER hev a place thar. Thar was that thar wot she never had ez a little girl with me and the old woman, and that she couldn't find ez a grownd up girl in any boarding-school—the home of a child; that kind o' innocent foolish-ness that I sometimes reckon must hev slipped outer our emigrant wagon comin' across the plains, or got left behind at St. Joe. She was a grownd girl fit to marry afore she was a child. She had young fellers a-sparkin' her afore she ever played with 'em ez boy and girl. I don't mind tellin' you that it wern't in the natur of Blair Rawlins' darter to teach her own darter any better, for all she's been a mighty help to me. So if it's all the same to you, Mr. Ford, we won't talk about a grownd up school; I'd rather Cress be a little girl again among them other children. I should be a powerful sight more kam if I knowed that when I was away huntin' stock or fightin' stakes with them Harrisons, that she was a settin' there with them and the birds and the bees, and listenin' to them and to you. Mebbee there's been a little too many scrimmages goin' on round the ranch sence she's been a child; mebbee she orter know suthin' more of a man than a feller who sparks her and fights for her."

The master was silent. Had this dull, narrow-minded partisan stumbled upon a truth that had never dawned upon his own broader comprehension? Had this selfish savage and literally red-handed frontier brawler been moved by some dumb instinct of the power of gentleness to understand his daughter's needs better than he? For a moment he was staggered. Then he thought of Cressy's later flirtations with Joe Masters, and her concealment of their meeting from her mother. Had she deceived her father also? Or was not the father deceiving him with this alternate suggestion of threat and of kindliness—of power and weakness. He had heard of this cruel phase of Southwestern cunning before. With the feeble sophistry of the cynic he mistrusted the good his scepticism could not understand. Howbeit, glancing sideways at the slumbering savagery of the man beside him, and his wounded hand, he did not care to show his lack of confidence. He contented himself with that equally feeble resource of weak humanity in such cases—good-natured indifference. "All right," he said carelessly; "I'll see what can be done. But are you quite sure you are fit to go home alone? Shall I accompany you?" As McKinstry waived the suggestion with a gesture, he added lightly, as if to conclude the interview, "I'll report progress to you from time to time, if you like."

"To ME," emphasized McKinstry; "not over THAR," indicating the ranch. "But p'rhaps you wouldn't mind my ridin' by and lookin' in at the school-room winder onct in a while? Ah—you WOULD," he added, with the first deepening of color he had shown. "Well, never mind."

"You see it might distract the children from their lessons," explained the master gently, who had however contemplated with some concern the infinite delight which a glimpse of McKinstry's fiery and fatuous face at the window would awaken in Johnny Filgee's infant breast.

"Well, no matter!" returned McKinstry slowly. "Ye don't keer, I s'pose, to come over to the hotel and take suthin'? A julep or a smash?"

"I shouldn't think of keeping you a moment longer from Mrs. McKinstry," said the master, looking at his companion's wounded hand. "Thank you all the same. Good-by."

They shook hands, McKinstry transferring his rifle to the hollow of his elbow to offer his unwounded left. The master watched him slowly resume his way towards the ranch. Then with a half uneasy and half pleasurable sense that he had taken some step whose consequences were more important than he would at present understand, he turned in the opposite direction to the school-house. He was so preoccupied that it was not until he had nearly reached it that he remembered Uncle Ben. With an odd recollection of McKinstry's previous performance, he approached the school from the thicket in the rear and slipped noiselessly to the open window with the intention of looking in. But the school-house, far from exhibiting that "kam" and studious abstraction which had so touched the savage breast of McKinstry, was filled with the accents of youthful and unrestrained vituperation. The voice of Rupert Filgee came sharply to the master's astonished ears.

"You needn't try to play off Dobell or Mitchell on ME—you hear! Much YOU know of either, don't you? Look at that copy. If Johnny couldn't do better than that, I'd lick him. Of course it's the pen—it ain't your stodgy fingers—oh, no! P'r'aps you'd like to hev a few more boxes o' quills and gold pens and Gillott's best thrown in, for two bits a lesson? I tell you what! I'll throw up the contract in another minit! There goes another quill busted! Look here, what YOU want ain't a pen, but a clothes-pin and a split nail! That'll about jibe with your dilikit gait."

The master at once stepped to the window and, unobserved, took a quick survey of the interior. Following some ingenious idea of his own regarding fitness, the beautiful Filgee had induced Uncle Ben to seat himself on the floor before one of the smallest desks, presumably his brother's, in an attitude which, while it certainly gave him considerable elbow-room for those contortions common to immature penmanship, offered his youthful instructor a superior eminence, from which he hovered, occasionally swooping down upon his grown-up pupil like a mischievous but graceful jay. But Mr. Ford's most distinct impression was that, far from resenting the derogatory position and the abuse that accompanied it, Uncle Ben not only beamed upon his persecutor with unquenchable good humor, but with undisguised admiration, and showed not the slightest inclination to accept his proposed resignation.

"Go slow, Roop," he said cheerfully. "You was onct a boy yourself. Nat'rally I kalkilate to stand all the damages. You've got ter waste some powder over a blast like this yer, way down to the bed rock. Next time I'll bring my own pens."

"Do. Some from the Dobell school you uster go to," suggested the darkly ironical Rupert. "They was iron-clad injin-rubber, warn't they?"

"Never you mind wot they were," said Uncle Ben good-humoredly. "Look at that string of 'C's' in that line. There's nothing mean about THEM."

He put his pen between his teeth, raised himself slowly on his legs, and shading his eyes with his hand from the severe perspective of six feet, gazed admiringly down upon his work. Rupert, with his hands in his pockets and his back to the window, cynically assisted at the inspection.

"Wot's that sick worm at the bottom of the page?" he asked.

"Wot might you think it wos?" said Uncle Ben beamingly.

"Looks like one o' them snake roots you dig up with a little mud stuck to it," returned Rupert critically.

"That's my name."

They both stood looking at it with their heads very much on one side. "It ain't so bad as the rest you've done. It MIGHT be your name. That ez, it don't look like anythin' else," suggested Rupert, struck with a new idea that it was perhaps more professional occasionally to encourage his pupil. "You might get on in course o' time. But what are you doin' all this for?" he asked suddenly.

"Doin' what?"

"This yer comin' to school when you ain't sent, and you ain't got no call to go—you, a grown-up man!"

The color deepened in Uncle Ben's face to the back of his ears. "Wot would you giv' to know, Roop? S'pose I reckoned some day to make a strike and sorter drop inter saciety easy—eh? S'pose I wanted to be ready to keep up my end with the other fellers, when the time kem? To be able to sling po'try and read novels and sich—eh?"

An expression of infinite and unutterable scorn dawned in the eyes of Rupert. "You do? Well," he repeated with slow and cutting deliberation, "I'll tell you what you're comin' here for, and the only thing that makes you come."

"What?"

"It's—some—girl!"

Uncle Ben broke into a boisterous laugh that made the roof shake, stamping about and slapping his legs till the crazy floor trembled. But at that moment the master stepped to the perch and made a quiet but discomposing entrance.

CHAPTER IV

The return of Miss Cressida McKinstry to Indian Spring and her interrupted studies was an event whose effects were not entirely confined to the school. The broken engagement itself seemed of little moment in the general estimation compared to her resumption of her old footing as a scholar. A few ill-natured elders of her own sex, and naturally exempt from the discriminating retort of Mr. McKinstry's "shot-gun," alleged that the Seminary at Sacramento had declined to receive her, but the majority accepted her return with local pride as a practical compliment to the educational facilities of Indian Spring. The Tuolumne "Star," with a breadth and eloquence touchingly disproportionate to its actual size and quality of type and paper, referred to the possible "growth of a grove of Academus at Indian Spring, under whose cloistered boughs future sages and statesmen were now meditating," in a way that made the master feel exceedingly uncomfortable. For some days the trail between the McKinstrys' ranch and the school-house was lightly patrolled by reliefs of susceptible young men, to whom the enfranchised Cressida, relieved from the dangerous supervision of the Davis-McKinstry clique, was an object of ambitious admiration. The young girl herself, who, in spite of the master's annoyance, seemed to be following some conscientious duty in consecutively arraying herself in the different dresses she had bought, however she may have tantalized her admirers by this revelation of bridal finery, did not venture to bring them near the limits of the play-ground. It struck the master with some surprise that Indian Spring did not seem to trouble itself in regard to his own privileged relations with its rustic enchantress; the young men clearly were not jealous of him; no matron had suggested any indecorum in a young girl of Cressy's years and antecedents being intrusted to the teachings of a young man scarcely her senior. Notwith-standing the attitude which Mr. Ford had been pleased to assume towards her, this implied compliment to his supposed monastic vocations affected him almost as uncomfortably as the "Star's" extravagant eulogium. He was obliged to recall certain foolish experiences of his own to enable him to rise superior to this presumption of his asceticism.

In pursuance of his promise to McKinstry, he had procured a few elementary books of study suitable to Cressy's new position, without, however, taking her out of the smaller classes or the discipline of the school. In a few weeks he was enabled to further improve her attitude by making her a "monitor" over the smaller girls, thereby dividing certain functions with Rupert Filgee, whose ministrations to the deceitful and "silly" sex had been characterized by perhaps more vigilant scorn and disparagement than was necessary. Cressy had accepted it as she had accepted her new studies, with an indolent good-humor, and at times a frankly supreme ignorance of their abstract or moral purpose that was discouraging. "What's the good of that?" she would ask, lifting her eyes abruptly to the master. Mr. Ford, somewhat embarrassed by her look, which always, sooner or later, frankly confessed itself an excuse for a perfectly irrelevant examination of his features in detail, would end in giving her some severely practical answer. Yet, if the subject appealed to any particular idiosyncrasy of her own, she would speedily master the study. A passing predilection for botany was provoked by a single incident. The master deeming this study a harmless young-lady-like occupation, had one day introduced the topic at recess, and was met by the usual answer. "But suppose," he continued artfully, "somebody sent you anonymously some flowers."

"Her ho!" suggested Johnny Filgee hoarsely, with bold bad recklessness. Ignoring the remark and the kick with which Rupert had resented it on the person of his brother, the master continued:

"And if you couldn't find out who sent them, you would want at least to know what they were and where they grew."

"Ef they grew anywhere 'bout yer we could tell her that," said a chorus of small voices.

The master hesitated. He was conscious of being on delicate ground. He was surrounded by a dozen pairs of little keen eyes from whom Nature had never yet succeeded in hiding her secrets—eyes that had waited for and knew the coming up of the earliest flowers; little fingers that had never turned the pages of a text-book, but knew where to scrape away the dead leaves above the first anemone, or had groped painfully among the lifeless branches in forgotten hollows for the shy dog-rose; unguided little feet that had instinctively made their way to remote southern slopes for the first mariposas, or had unerringly threaded the tule-hidden banks of the river for flower-de-luce. Convinced that he could not hold his own on their level, he shamelessly struck at once above it.

"Suppose that one of those flowers," he continued, "was not like the rest; that its stalks and leaves, instead of being green and soft, were white and stringy like flannel as if to protect it from cold, wouldn't it be nice to be able to say at once that it had lived only in the snow, and that some one must have gone all that way up there above the snow line to pick it?"

The children, taken aback by this unfair introduction of a floral stranger, were silent. Cressy thoughtfully accepted botany on those possibilities. A week later she laid on the master's desk a limp-looking plant with a stalk like heavy frayed worsted yarn. "It ain't much to look at after all, is it?" she said. "I reckon I could cut a better one with scissors outer an old cloth jacket of mine."

"And you found it here?" asked the master in surprise.

"I got Masters to look for it when he was on the Summit. I described it to him. I didn't allow he had the gumption to get it. But he did."

Although botany languished slightly after this vicarious effort, it kept Cressy in fresh bouquets, and extending its gentle influence to her friends and acquaintances became slightly confounded with horticulture, led to the planting of one or two gardens, and was accepted in school as an implied concession to berries, apples, and nuts. In reading and writing Cressy greatly improved, with a marked decrease in grammatical solecisms, although she still retained certain characteristic words, and always her own slow Southwestern, half musical intonation. This languid deliberation was particularly noticeable in her reading aloud, and gave the studied and measured rhetoric a charm of which her careless colloquial speech was incapable. Even the "Fifth Reader," with its imposing passages from the English classics carefully selected with a view of paralyzing small, hesitating, or hurried voices, in Cressy's hands became no longer an unintelligible incantation. She had quietly mastered the difficulties of pronunciation by some instinctive sense of euphony if not of comprehension. The master with his eyes closed hardly recognized his pupil. Whether or not she understood what she read he hesitated to inquire; no doubt, as with her other studies, she knew what attracted her.

Rupert Filgee, a sympathetic if not always a correct reader, who boldly took four and five syllabled fences flying only to come to grief perhaps in the ditch of some rhetorical pause beyond, alone expressed his scorn of her performance. Octavia Dean, torn between her hopeless affection for this beautiful but inaccessible boy, and her soul-friendship for this bigger but many-frocked girl, studied the master's face with watchful anxiety.

It is needless to say that Hiram McKinstry was, in the intervals of stake-driving and stock-hunting, heavily contented with this latest evidence of his daughter's progress. He even intimated to the master that her reading being an accomplishment that could be exercised at home was conducive to that "kam" in which he was so deficient. It was also rumored that Cressy's oral rendering of Addison's "Reflections in Westminster Abbey" and Burke's "Indictment of Warren Hastings," had beguiled him one evening from improving an opportunity to "plug" one of Harrison's boundary "raiders."

The master shared in Cressy's glory in the public eye. But although Mrs. McKinstry did not materially change her attitude of tolerant good-nature towards him, he was painfully conscious that she looked upon her daughter's studies and her husband's interests in them as a weakness that might in course of time produce infirmity of homicidal purpose and become enervating of eye and trigger-finger. And when Mr. McKinstry got himself appointed as school-trustee, and was thereby obliged to mingle with certain Eastern settlers,—colleagues on the Board,—this possible weakening of the old sharply drawn sectional line between "Yanks" and themselves gave her grave doubts of Hiram's physical stamina.

"The old man's worrits hev sorter shook out a little of his

sand," she had explained. On those evenings when he attended the Board, she sought higher consolation in prayer meeting at the Southern Baptist Church, in whose exercises her Northern and Eastern neighbors, thinly disguised as "Baal" and "Astaroth," were generally overthrown and their temples made desolate.

If Uncle Ben's progress was slower, it was no less satisfactory. Without imagination and even without enthusiasm, he kept on with a dull laborious persistency. When the irascible impatience of Rupert Filgee at last succumbed to the obdurate slowness of his pupil, the master himself, touched by Uncle Ben's perspiring forehead and perplexed eyebrows, often devoted the rest of the afternoon to a gentle elucidation of the mysteries before him, setting copies for his heavy hand, or even guiding it with his own, like a child's, across the paper. At times the appalling uselessness of Uncle Ben's endeavors reminded him of Rupert's taunting charge. Was he really doing this from a genuine thirst for knowledge? It was inconsistent with all that Indian Spring knew of his antecedents and his present ambitions; he was a simple miner without scientific or technical knowledge; his already slight acquaintance with arithmetic and the scrawl that served for his signature were more than sufficient for his needs. Yet it was with this latter sign-manual that he seemed to take infinite pains. The master, one afternoon, thought fit to correct the apparent vanity of this performance.

"If you took as much care in trying to form your letters according to copy, you'd do better. Your signature is fair enough as it is."

"But it don't look right, Mr. Ford," said Uncle Ben, eying it distrustfully; "somehow it ain't all there."

"Why, certainly it is. Look, D A B N E Y—not very plain, it's true, but there are all the letters."

"That's just it, Mr. Ford; them AIN'T all the letters that ORTER be there. I've allowed to write it D A B N E Y to save time and ink, but it orter read DAUBIGNY," said Uncle Ben, with painful distinctness.

"But that spells d'Aubigny!"

"It are."

"Is that your name?"

"I reckon."

The master looked at Uncle Ben doubtfully. Was this only another form of the Dobell illusion? "Was your father a Frenchman?" he asked finally.

Uncle Ben paused as if to recall the trifling circumstances of his father's nationality. "No."

"Your grandfather?"

"I reckon not. At least ye couldn't prove it by me."

"Was your father or grandfather a voyageur or trapper, or Canadian?"

"They were from Pike County, Mizzoori."

The master regarded Uncle Ben still dubiously. "But you call yourself Dabney. What makes you think your real name is d'Aubigny?"

"That's the way it uster be writ in letters to me in the States. Hold on. I'll show ye." He deliberately began to feel in his pockets, finally extracting his old purse from which he produced a crumpled envelope, and carefully smoothing it out, compared it with his signature.

"Thar, you see. It's the same—d'Aubigny."

The master hesitated. After all, it was not impossible. He recalled other instances of the singular transformation of names in the Californian emigration. Yet he could not help saying, "Then you concluded d'Aubigny was a better name than Dabney?"

"Do YOU think it's better?"

"Women might. I dare say your wife would prefer to be called Mrs. d'Aubigny rather than Dabney."

The chance shot told. Uncle Ben suddenly flushed to his ears.

"I didn't think o' that," he said hurriedly. "I had another idee. I reckoned that on the matter o' holdin' property and passin' in money it would be better to hev your name put on the square, and to sorter go down to bed rock for it, eh? If I wanted to take a hand in them lots or Ditch shares, for instance—it would be only law to hev it made out in the name o' d'Aubigny."

Mr. Ford listened with certain impatient contempt. It was bad enough for Uncle Ben to have exposed his weakness in inventing fictions about his early education, but to invest himself now with a contingency of capital for the sake of another childish vanity, was pitiable as it was preposterous. There was no doubt that he had lied about his school experiences; it was barely probable that his name was really d'Aubigny, and it was quite consistent with all this—even setting apart the fact that he was perfectly well known to be only a poor miner—that he should lie again. Like most logical reasoners Mr. Ford forgot that humanity might be illogical and inconsistent without being insincere. He turned away without speaking as if indicating a wish to hear no more.

"Some o' these days," said Uncle Ben, with dull persistency, "I'll tell ye suthen'."

"I'd advise you just now to drop it and stick to your lessons," said the master sharply.

"That's so," said Uncle Ben hurriedly, hiding himself as it were in an all-encompassing blush. "In course lessons first, boys, that's the motto." He again took up his pen and assumed his old laborious attitude. But after a few moments it became evident that either the master's curt dismissal of his subject or his own preoccupation with it, had somewhat unsettled him. He cleaned his pen obtrusively, going to the window for a better light, and whistling from time to time with a demonstrative carelessness and a depressing gayety. He once broke into a murmuring, meditative chant evidently referring to the previous conversation, in its—"That's so— Yer we go—Lessons the first, boys, Yo, heave O." The rollicking marine character of this refrain, despite its utter incongruousness, apparently struck him favorably, for he repeated it softly, occasionally glancing behind him at the master who was coldly absorbed at his desk. Presently he arose, carefully put his books away, symmetrically piling them in a pyramid beside Mr. Ford's motionless elbow, and then lifting his feet with high but gentle steps went to the peg where his coat and hat were hanging. As he was about to put them on he appeared suddenly struck with a sense of indecorousness in dressing himself in the school, and taking them on his arm to the porch resumed them outside. Then saying, "I clean disremembered I'd got to see a man. So long, till to-morrow," he disappeared whistling softly.

The old woodland hush fell back upon the school. It seemed very quiet and empty. A faint sense of remorse stole over the master. Yet he remembered that Uncle Ben had accepted without reproach and as a good joke much more direct accusations from Rupert Filgee, and that he himself had acted from a conscientious sense of duty towards the man. But a conscientious sense of duty to inflict pain upon a fellow-mortal for his own good does not always bring perfect serenity to the inflicter—possibly because, in the defective machinery of human compensation, pain is the only quality that is apt to appear in the illustration. Mr. Ford felt uncomfortable, and being so, was naturally vexed at the innocent cause. Why should Uncle Ben be offended because he had simply declined to follow his weak fabrications any further? This was his return for having tolerated it at first! It would be a lesson to him henceforth. Nevertheless he got up and went to the door. The figure of Uncle Ben was already indistinct among the leaves, but from the motion of his shoulders he seemed to be still stepping high and softly as if not yet clear of insecure and engulfing ground.

The silence still continuing, the master began mechanically to look over the desks for forgotten or mislaid articles, and to rearrange the pupils' books and copies. A few heartsease gathered by the devoted Octavia Dean, neatly tied with a black thread and regularly left in the inkstand cavity of Rupert's desk, were still lying on the floor where they had been always hurled with equal regularity by that disdainful Adonis. Picking up a slate from under a bench, his attention was attracted by a forgotten cartoon on the reverse side. Mr. Ford at once recognized it as the work of that youthful but eminent caricaturist, Johnny Filgee. Broad in treatment, comprehensive in subject, liberal in detail and slate-pencil— it represented Uncle Ben lying on the floor with a book in his hand, tyrannized over by Rupert Filgee and regarded in a striking profile of two features by Cressy McKinstry. The daring realism of introducing the names of each character on their legs—perhaps ideally enlarged for that purpose—left no doubt of their identity. Equally daring but no less effective was the rendering of a limited but dramatic conversation between the parties by the aid of emotional balloons attached to their mouths like a visible gulp bearing the respective legends: "I luv you," "O my," and "You git!"

The master was for a moment startled at this unlooked-for but graphic testimony to the fact that Uncle Ben's visits to the school were not only known but commented upon. The small eyes of those youthful observers had been keener than his own. He had again been stupidly deceived, in spite of his efforts. Love, albeit deficient in features and wearing an improperly short bell-shaped frock, had boldly re-entered the peaceful school, and disturbing complications on abnormal legs were following at its heels.

CHAPTER V

While this simple pastoral life was centred around the school-house in the clearing, broken only by an occasional warning pistol-shot in the direction of the Harrison-McKinstry boundaries, the more business part of Indian Spring was overtaken by one of those spasms of enterprise peculiar to all Californian mining settlements. The opening of the Eureka Ditch and the extension of stagecoach communication from Big Bluff were events of no small importance, and were celebrated on the same day. The double occasion overtaxing even the fluent rhetoric of the editor of the "Star" left him struggling in the metaphorical difficulties of a Pactolian Spring, which he had rashly turned into the Ditch, and obliged him to transfer the onerous duty of writing the editorial on the Big Bluff Extension to the hands of the Honorable Abner Dean, Assemblyman from Angel's. The loss of the Honorable Mr. Dean's right eye in an early pioneer fracas did not prevent him from looking into the dim vista of the future and discovering with that single unaided optic enough to fill three columns of the "Star." "It is not too extravagant to say," he remarked with charming deprecation, "that Indian Spring, through its own perfectly organized system of inland transportation, the confluence of its North Fork with the Sacramento River, and their combined effluence into the illimitable Pacific, is thus put not only into direct communication with far Cathay but even remoter Antipodean markets. The citizen of Indian Spring taking the 9 A. M. Pioneer Coach and arriving at Big Bluff at 2.40 is enabled to connect with the through express to Sacramento the same evening, reaching San Francisco per the Steam Navigation Company's palatial steamers in time to take the Pacific Mail Steamer to Yokohama on the following day at 8.30 P. M." Although no citizen of Indian Spring appeared to avail himself of this admirable opportunity, nor did it appear at all likely that any would, everybody vaguely felt that an inestimable boon lay in the suggestion, and even the master professionally intrusting the reading aloud of the editorial to Rupert Filgee with ulterior designs of practice in the pronunciation of five-syllable words, was somewhat affected by it. Johnny Filgee and Jimmy Snyder accepting it as a mysterious something that made Desert Islands accessible at a moment's notice and a trifling outlay, were round-eyed and attentive. And the culminating information from the master that this event would be commemorated by a half-holiday, combined to make the occasion as exciting to the simple school-house in the clearing as it was to the gilded saloon in the main street.

And so the momentous day arrived, with its two new coaches from Big Bluff containing the specially invited speakers— always specially invited to those occasions, and yet strangely enough never before feeling the extreme "importance and privilege" of it as they did then. Then there were the firing of two anvils, the strains of a brass band, the hoisting of a new flag on the liberty-pole, and later the ceremony of the Ditch opening, when a distinguished speaker in a most unworkman-like tall hat, black frock coat, and white cravat, which gave him the general air of a festive grave-digger, took a spade from the hands of an apparently hilarious chief mourner and threw out the first sods. There were anvils, brass bands, and a "collation" at the hotel. But everywhere— overriding the most extravagant expectation and even the laughter it provoked—the spirit of indomitable youth and resistless enterprise intoxicated the air. It was the spirit that had made California possible; that had sown a thousand such ventures broadcast through its wilderness; that had enabled the sower to stand half-humorously among his scant or ruined harvests without fear and without repining, and turn his undaunted and ever hopeful face to further fields. What mattered it that Indian Spring had always before its eyes the abandoned trenches and ruined outworks of its earlier pioneers? What mattered it that the eloquent eulogist of the Eureka Ditch had but a few years before as prodigally scattered his adjectives and his fortune on the useless tunnel that confronted him on the opposite side of the river? The sublime forgetfulness of youth ignored its warning or recognized it as a joke. The master, fresh from his little flock and prematurely aged by their contact, felt a stirring of something like envy as he wandered among these scarcely older enthusiasts.

Especially memorable was the exciting day to Johnny Filgee, not only for the delightfully bewildering clamor of the brass band, in which, between the trombone and the bass drum, he had got inextricably mixed; not only for the half-frightening explosions of the anvils and the maddening smell of the gunpowder which had exalted his infant soul to sudden and irrelevant whoopings, but for a singular occurrence that whetted his always keen perceptions. Having been shamelessly abandoned on the veranda of the Eureka Hotel while his brother Rupert paid bashful court to the pretty proprietress by assisting her in her duties, Johnny gave himself up to unlimited observation. The rosettes of the six horses, the new harness, the length of the driver's whiplash, his enormous buckskin gloves and the way he held his reins; the fascinating odor of shining varnish on the coach, the gold-headed cane of the Honorable Abner Dean: all these were stored away in the secret recesses of Johnny's memory, even as the unconsidered trifles he had picked up en route were distending his capacious pockets. But when a young man had alighted from the second or "Truly" coach among the REAL passengers, and strolled carelessly and easily in the veranda as if the novelty and the occasion were nothing to him, Johnny, with a gulp of satisfaction, knew that he had seen a prince! Beautifully dressed in a white duck suit, with a diamond ring on his finger, a gold chain swinging from his fob, and a Panama hat with a broad black ribbon jauntily resting on his curled and scented hair, Johnny's eyes had never rested on a more resplendent vision. He was more romantic than Yuba Bill, more imposing and less impossible than the Honorable Abner Dean, more eloquent than the master—far more beautiful than any colored print that he had ever seen. Had he brushed him in passing Johnny would have felt a thrill; had he spoken to him he knew he would have been speechless to reply. Judge then of his utter stupefaction when he saw Uncle Ben—actually Uncle Ben!—approach this paragon of perfection, albeit with some embarrassment, and after a word or two of unintelligible conversation walk away with him! Need it be wondered that Johnny, forgetful at once of his brother, the horses, and even the collation with its possible "goodies," instantly followed.

The two men turned into the side street, which, after a few hundred yards, opened upon the deserted mining flat, crossed and broken by the burrows and mounds made by the forgotten engines of the early gold-seekers. Johnny, at times hidden by these irregularities, kept closely in their rear, sauntering whenever he came within the range of their eyes in that sidelong, spasmodic and generally diagonal fashion peculiar to small boys, but ready at any moment to assume utter unconsciousness and the appearance of going somewhere else or of searching for something on the ground. In this way appearing, if noticed at all, each time in some different position to the right or left of them, Johnny followed them to the fringe of woodland which enabled him to draw closer to their heels.

Utterly oblivious of this artistic "shadowing" in the insignificant person of the small boy who once or twice even crossed their path with affected timidity, they continued an apparently confidential previous interview. The words "stocks" and "shares" were alone intelligible. Johnny had heard them during the day, but he was struck by the fact that Uncle Ben seemed to be seeking information from the paragon and was perfectly submissive and humble. But the boy was considerably mystified when after a tramp of half an hour they arrived upon the debatable ground of the Harrison-McKinstry boundary. Having been especially warned never to go there, Johnny as a matter of course was perfectly familiar with it. But what was the incomprehensible stranger doing there? Was he brought by Uncle Ben with a view of paralyzing both of the combatants with the spectacle of his perfections? Was he a youthful sheriff, a young judge, or maybe the son of the Governor of California? Or was it that Uncle Ben was "silly" and didn't know the locality? Here was an opportunity for him, Johnny, to introduce himself, and explain and even magnify the danger, with perhaps a slight allusion to his own fearless familiarity with it. Unfortunately, as he was making up his small mind behind a tree, the paragon turned and with the easy disdain that so well became him, said:

"Well, I wouldn't offer a dollar an acre for the whole ranch. But if YOU choose to give a fancy price—that's your lookout."

To Johnny's already prejudiced mind, Uncle Ben received this just contempt submissively, as he ought, but nevertheless he muttered something "silly" in reply, which Johnny was really too disgusted to listen to. Ought he not to step forward and inform the paragon that he was wasting his time on a man who couldn't even spell "ba-ker," and who was taught his letters by his, Johnny's, brother?

The paragon continued:

"And of course you know that merely your buying the title to the land don't give you possession. You'll have to fight these squatters and jumpers just the same. It'll be three instead of two fighting—that's all!"

Uncle Ben's imbecile reply did not trouble Johnny. He had ears now only for the superior intellect before him. IT continued coolly:

"Now let's take a look at that yield of yours. I haven't much time to give you, as I expect some men to be looking for me here—and I suppose you want this thing still kept a secret. I don't see how you've managed to do it so far. Is your claim near? You live on it—I think you said?"

But that the little listener was so preoccupied with the stranger, this suggestion of Uncle Ben's having a claim worth the attention of that distinguished presence would have set him thinking; the little that he understood he set down to Uncle Ben's "gassin'." As the two men moved forward again, he followed them until Uncle Ben's house was reached.

It was a rude shanty of boards and rough boulders, half burrowing in one of the largest mounds of earth and gravel, which had once represented the tailings or refuse of the abandoned Indian Spring Placer. In fact it was casually alleged by some that Uncle Ben eked out the scanty "grub wages," he made by actual mining, in reworking and sifting the tailings at odd times—a degrading work hitherto practised only by Chinese, and unworthy the Caucasian ambition. The mining code of honor held that a man might accept the smallest results of his daily labor, as long as he was sustained by the prospect of a larger "strike," but condemned his contentment with a modest certainty. Nevertheless a little of this suspicion encompassed his dwelling and contributed to its loneliness, even as a long ditch, the former tail-race of the claim, separated him from his neighbors. Prudently halting at the edge of the wood, Johnny saw his resplendent vision cross the strip of barren flat, and enter the cabin with Uncle Ben like any other mortal. He sat down on a stump and awaited its return, which he fondly hoped might be alone! At the end of half an hour he made a short excursion to examine the condition of a blackberry bramble, and returned to his post of observation. But there was neither sound nor motion in the direction of the cabin. When another ten minutes had elapsed, the door opened and to Johnny's intense discomfiture, Uncle Ben appeared alone and walked leisurely towards the woods. Burning with anxiety Johnny threw himself in Uncle Ben's way. But here occurred one of those surprising inconsistencies known only to children. As Uncle Ben turned his small gray eyes upon him in a half astonished, half questioning manner, the potent spirit of childish secretiveness suddenly took possession of the boy. Wild horses could not now have torn from him that question which only a moment before was on his lips.

"Hullo, Johnny! What are ye doin' here?" said Uncle Ben kindly.

"Nothin'." After a pause, in which he walked all round Uncle Ben's large figure, gazing up at him as if he were a monument, he added, "Huntin' blackberrieth."

"Why ain't you over at the collation?"

"Ruperth there," he answered promptly.

The idea of being thus vicariously present in the person of his brother seemed a sufficient excuse. He leap-frogged over the stump on which he had been sitting as an easy unembarrassing pause for the next question. But Uncle Ben was apparently perfectly satisfied with Johnny's reply, and nodding to him, walked away.

When his figure had disappeared in the bushes, Johnny cautiously approached the cabin. At a certain distance he picked up a stone and threw it against the door, immediately taking to his heels and the friendly copse again. No one appearing he repeated the experiment twice and even thrice with a larger stone and at a nearer distance. Then he boldly skirted the cabin and dropped into the race-way at its side. Following it a few hundred yards he came upon a long disused shaft opening into it, which had been covered with a rough trap of old planks, as if to protect incautious wayfarers from falling in. Here a sudden and inexplicable fear overtook Johnny, and he ran away. When he reached the hotel, almost the first sight that met his astounded eyes was the spectacle of the paragon, apparently still in undisturbed possession of all his perfections—driving coolly off in a buggy with a fresh companion.

Meantime Mr. Ford, however touched by the sentimental significance of the celebration, became slightly wearied of its details. As his own room in the Eureka Hotel was actually thrilled by the brass band without and the eloquence of speakers below, and had become redolent of gunpowder and champagne exploded around it, he determined to return to the school-house and avail himself of its woodland quiet to write a few letters.

The change was grateful, the distant murmur of the excited

settlement came only as the soothing sound of wind among the leaves. The pure air of the pines that filled every cranny of the quiet school-room, and seemed to disperse all taint of human tenancy, made the far-off celebrations as unreal as a dream. The only reality of his life was here.

He took from his pocket a few letters one of which was worn and soiled with frequent handling. He re-read it in a half methodical, half patient way, as if he were waiting for some revelation it inspired, which was slow that afternoon in coming. At other times it had called up a youthful enthusiasm which was wont to transfigure his grave and prematurely reserved face with a new expression. To-day the revelation and expression were both wanting. He put the letter back with a slight sigh, that sounded so preposterous in the silent room that he could not forego an embarrassed smile. But the next moment he set himself seriously to work on his correspondence.

Presently he stopped; once or twice he had been overtaken by a vague undefinable sense of pleasure, even to the dreamy halting of his pen. It was a sensation in no way connected with the subject of his correspondence, or even his previous reflections—it was partly physical, and yet it was in some sense suggestive. It must be the intoxicating effect of the woodland air. He even fancied he had noticed it before, at the same hour when the sun was declining and the fresh odors of the undergrowth were rising. It certainly was a perfume. He raised his eyes. There lay the cause on the desk before him—a little nosegay of wild Californian myrtle encircling a rose-bud which had escaped his notice.

There was nothing unusual in the circumstance. The children were in the habit of making their offerings generally without particular reference to time or occasion, and it might have been overlooked by him during school-hours. He felt a pity for the forgotten posy already beginning to grow limp in its neglected solitude. He remembered that in some folk-lore of the children's, perhaps a tradition of the old association of the myrtle with Venus, it was believed to be emblematic of the affections. He remembered also that he had even told them of this probable origin of their superstition. He was still holding it in his hand when he was conscious of a silken sensation that sent a magnetic thrill through his fingers. Looking at it more closely he saw that the sprigs were bound together, not by thread or ribbon, but by long filaments of soft brown hair tightly wound around them. He unwound a single hair and held it to the light. Its length, color, texture, and above all a certain inexplicable instinct, told him it was Cressy McKinstry's. He laid it down quickly, as if he had, in that act, familiarly touched her person.

He finished his letter, but presently found himself again looking at the myrtle and thinking about it. From the position in which it had been placed it was evidently intended for him; the fancy of binding it with hair was also intentional and not a necessity, as he knew his feminine scholars were usually well provided with bits of thread, silk, or ribbon. If it had been some new absurdity of childish fashion introduced in the school, he would have noticed it ere this. For it was this obtrusion of a personality that vaguely troubled him. He remembered Cressy's hair; it was certainly very beautiful, in spite of her occasional vagaries of coiffure. He recalled how, one afternoon, it had come down when she was romping with Octavia in the play-ground, and was surprised to find what a vivid picture he retained of her lingering in the porch to put it up; her rounded arms held above her head, her pretty shoulders, full throat, and glowing face thrown back, and a wisp of the very hair between her white teeth! He began another letter.

When it was finished the shadow of the pine-branch before

the window, thrown by the nearly level sun across his paper, had begun slowly to reach the opposite wall. He put his work away, lingered for a moment in hesitation over the myrtle sprays, and then locked them in his desk with an odd feeling that he had secured in some vague way a hold upon Cressy's future vagaries; then reflecting that Uncle Ben, whom he had seen in town, would probably keep holiday with the others, he resolved to wait no longer, but strolled back to the hotel. The act however had not recalled Uncle Ben to him by any association of ideas, for since his discovery of Johnny Filgee's caricature he had failed to detect anything to corroborate the caricaturist's satire, and had dismissed the subject from his mind.

On entering his room at the hotel he found Rupert Filgee standing moodily by the window, while his brother Johnny, overcome by a repletion of excitement and collation, was asleep on the single arm-chair. Their presence was not unusual, as Mr. Ford, touched by the loneliness of these motherless boys, had often invited them to come to his rooms to look over his books and illustrated papers.

"Well?" he said cheerfully.

Rupert did not reply or change his position. Mr. Ford, glancing at him sharply, saw a familiar angry light in the boy's beautiful eyes, slightly dimmed by a tear. Laying his hand gently on Rupert's shoulder he said, "What's the matter, Rupert?"

"Nothin'," said the boy doggedly, with his eyes still fixed on the pane.

"Has—has—Mrs. Tripp" (the fair proprietress) "been unkind?" he went on lightly.

No reply.

"You know, Rupe," continued Mr. Ford demurely, "she must show SOME reserve before company—like to-day. It won't do to make a scandal."

Rupert maintained an indignant silence. But the dimple (which he usually despised as a feminine blot) on the cheek nearer the master became slightly accented. Only for a moment; the dark eyes clouded again.

"I wish I was dead, Mr. Ford."

"Hallo!"

"Or—doin' suthin'."

"That's better. What do you want to do?"

"To work—make a livin' myself. Quit toten' wood and water at home; quit cookin' and makin' beds, like a yaller Chinaman; quit nussin' babies and dressin' 'em and undressin' 'em, like a girl. Look at HIM now," pointing to the sweetly unconscious Johnny, "look at him there. Do you know what that means? It means I've got to pack him home through the town jist ez he is thar, and then make a fire and bile his food for him, and wash him and undress him and put him to bed, and 'Now I lay me down to sleep' him, and tuck him up; and Dad all the while 'scootin' round town with other idjits, jawin' about 'progress' and the 'future of Injin Spring.' Much future we've got over our own house, Mr. Ford. Much future he's got laid up for me!"

The master, to whom those occasional outbreaks from Rupert were not unfamiliar, smiled, albeit with serious eyes that belied his lips, and consoled the boy as he had often done before. But he was anxious to know the cause of this recent attack and its probable relations to the fascinating Mrs. Tripp.

"I thought we talked all that over some time ago, Rupe. In a few months you'll be able to leave school, and I'll advise your father about putting you into something to give you a chance for yourself. Patience, old fellow; you're doing very well. Consider—there's your pupil, Uncle Ben."

"Oh, yes! That's another big baby to tot round in school when I ain't niggerin' at home."

"And I don't see exactly what else you could do at Indian Spring," continued Mr. Ford.

"No," said Rupert gloomily, "but I could get away to Sacramento. Yuba Bill says they take boys no bigger nor me in thar express offices or banks—and in a year or two they're as good ez anybody and get paid as big. Why, there was a fellow here, just now, no older than you, Mr. Ford, and not half your learnin', and he dressed to death with jewelry, and everybody bowin' and scrapin' to him, that it was perfectly sickenin'."

Mr. Ford lifted his eyebrows. "Oh, you mean the young man of Benham and Co., who was talking to Mrs. Tripp?" he said.

A quick flush of angry consciousness crossed Rupert's face. "Maybe; he has just cheek enough for anythin'."

"And you want to be like him?" said Mr. Ford.

"You know what I mean, Mr. Ford. Not LIKE him. Why YOU'RE as good as he is, any day," continued Rupert with relentless naivete; "but if a jay-bird like that can get on, why couldn't I?"

There was no doubt that the master here pointed out the defectiveness of Rupert's logic and the beneficence of patience and study, as became their relations of master and pupil, but with the addition of a certain fellow sympathy and some amusing recital of his own boyish experiences, that had the effect of calling Rupert's dimples into action again. At the end of half an hour the boy had become quite tractable, and, getting ready to depart, approached his sleeping brother with something like resignation. But Johnny's nap seemed to have had the effect of transforming him into an inert jelly-like mass. It required the joint exertions of both the master and Rupert to transfer him bodily into the latter's arms, where, with a single limp elbow encircling his brother's neck, he lay with his unfinished slumber still visibly distending his cheeks, his eyelids, and even lifting his curls from his moist forehead. The master bade Rupert "good-night," and returned to his room as the boy descended the stairs with his burden.

But here Providence, with, I fear, its occasional disregard of mere human morality, rewarded Rupert after his own foolish desires. Mrs. Tripp was at the foot of the stairs as Rupert came slowly down. He saw her, and was covered with shame; she saw him and his burden, and was touched with kindliness. Whether or not she was also mischievously aware of Rupert's admiration, and was not altogether displeased with it, I cannot say. In a voice that thrilled him, she said:—

"What! Rupert, are you going so soon?"

"Yes, ma'am—on account of Johnny."

"But let me take him—I can keep him here to-night."

It was a great temptation, but Rupert had strength to refuse, albeit with his hat pulled over his downcast eyes.

"Poor dear, how tired he looks."

She approached her still fresh and pretty face close to Rupert and laid her lips on Johnny's cheek. Then she lifted her audacious eyes to his brother, and pushing back his well-worn chip hat from his clustering curls, she kissed him squarely on the forehead.

"Good-night, dear."

The boy stumbled, and then staggered blindly forward into the outer darkness. But with a gentleman's delicacy he turned almost instantly into a side street, as if to keep this consecration of himself from vulgar eyes. The path he had chosen was rough and weary, the night was dark, and Johnny was ridiculously heavy, but he kept steadily on, the woman's kiss in the fancy of the foolish boy shining on his forehead and lighting him onward like a star.

CHAPTER VI

When the door closed on Rupert the master pulled down the blind, and, trimming his lamp, tried to compose himself by reading. Outside, the "Great Day for Indian Spring" was slowly evaporating in pale mists from the river, and the celebration itself spasmodically taking flight here and there in Roman candles and rockets. An occasional outbreak from revellers in the bar-room below, a stumbling straggler along the planked sidewalk before the hotel, only seemed to intensify the rustic stillness. For the future of Indian Spring was still so remote that Nature insensibly re-invested its boundaries on the slightest relaxation of civic influence, and Mr. Ford lifted his head from the glowing columns of the "Star" to listen to the far-off yelp of a coyote on the opposite shore.

He was also conscious of the recurrence of that vague, pleasurable recollection, so indefinite that, when he sought to identify it with anything—even the finding of the myrtle sprays on his desk—it evaded him. He tried to work, with the same interruption. Then an uneasy sensation that he had not been sufficiently kind to Rupert in his foolish love-troubles remorsefully seized him. A half pathetic, half humorous picture of the miserable Rupert staggering under the double burden of his sleeping brother and a misplaced affection, or possibly abandoning the one or both in the nearest ditch in a reckless access of boyish frenzy and fleeing his home forever, rose before his eyes. He seized his hat with the intention of seeking him—or forgetting him in some other occupation by the way. For Mr. Ford had the sensitive conscience of many imaginative people; an unfailing monitor, it was always calling his whole moral being into play to evade it.

As he crossed the passage he came upon Mrs. Tripp hooded and elaborately attired in a white ball dress, which however did not, to his own fancy, become her as well as her ordinary costume. He was passing her with a bow, when she said, with complacent consciousness of her appearance, "Aren't you going to the ball to-night?"

He remembered then that "an opening ball" at the Court-house was a part of the celebration. "No," he said smiling; "but it is a pity that Rupert couldn't have seen you in your charming array."

"Rupert," said the lady, with a slightly coquettish laugh; "you have made him as much a woman-hater as yourself. I offered to take him in our party, and he ran away to you." She paused, and giving him a furtive critical glance said, with an easy mingling of confidence and audacity, "Why don't YOU go? Nobody'll hurt you."

"I'm not so sure of that," replied Mr. Ford gallantly. "There's the melancholy example of Rupert always before me."

Mrs. Tripp tossed her chignon and descended a step of the stairs. "You'd better go," she continued, looking up over the balusters. "You can look on if you can't dance."

Now Mr. Ford COULD dance, and it so chanced, rather well, too. With this consciousness he remained standing in half indignant hesitation on the landing as she disappeared. Why shouldn't he go? It was true, he had half tacitly acquiesced in the reserve with which he had been treated, and had never mingled socially in the gatherings of either sex at Indian Spring—but that was no reason. He could at least dress himself, walk to the Court-house and—look on.

Any black coat and white shirt was sufficiently de rigueur for Indian Spring. Mr. Ford added the superfluous elegance of a forgotten white waistcoat. When he reached the sidewalk it was only nine o'clock, but the windows of the Court-house were already flaring like a stranded steamer on the barren bank where it had struck. On the way thither he was once or twice tempted to change his mind, and hesitated even at the very door. But the fear that his hesitation would be noticed by the few loungers before it, and the fact that some of them were already hesitating through bashfulness, determined him to enter.

The clerks' office and judges' chambers on the lower floor had been invaded by wraps, shawls, and refreshments, but the dancing was reserved for the upper floor or courtroom, still unfinished. Flags, laurel-wreaths, and appropriate floral inscriptions hid its bare walls; but the coat of arms of the State, already placed over the judges' dais with its illimitable golden sunset, its triumphant goddess, and its implacable grizzly, seemed figuratively to typify the occasion better than the inscriptions. The room was close and crowded. The flickering candles in tin sconces against the walls, or depending in rude chandeliers of barrel-hoops from the ceiling, lit up the most astounding diversity of female costume the master had ever seen. Gowns of bygone fashions, creased and stained with packing and disuse, toilets of forgotten festivity revised with modern additions; garments in and out of season—a fur-trimmed jacket and a tulle skirt, a velvet robe under a pique sacque; fresh young faces beneath faded head-dresses, and mature and buxom charms in virgin' white. The small space cleared for the dancers was continually invaded by the lookers-on, who in files of three deep lined the room.

As the master pushed his way to the front, a young girl, who had been standing in the sides of a quadrille, suddenly darted with a nymph-like quickness among the crowd and was for an instant hidden. Without distinguishing either face or figure, Mr. Ford recognized in the quick, impetuous action a characteristic movement of Cressy's; with an embarrassing instinct that he could not account for, he knew she had seen him, and that, for some inexplicable reason, he was the cause of her sudden disappearance.

But it was only for a moment. Even while he was vaguely scanning the crowd she reappeared and took her place beside her mystified partner—the fascinating stranger of Johnny's devotion and Rupert's dislike. She was pale; he had never seen her so beautiful. All that he had thought distasteful and incongruous in her were but accessories of her loveliness at that moment, in that light, in that atmosphere, in that strange assembly. Even her full pink gauze dress, from which her fair young shoulders slipped as from a sunset cloud, seemed only the perfection of virginal simplicity; her girlish length of limb and the long curves of her neck and back were now the outlines of thorough breeding. The absence of color in her usually fresh face had been replaced by a faint magnetic aurora that seemed to him half spiritual. He could not take his eyes from her; he could not believe what he saw. Yet that was Cressy McKinstry—his pupil! Had he ever really seen her? Did he know her now? Small wonder that all eyes were bent upon her, that a murmur of unspoken admiration, or still more intense hush of silence moved the people around him. He glanced hurriedly at them, and was oddly relieved by this evident participation in his emotions.

She was dancing now, and with that same pale restraint and curious quiet that had affected him so strongly. She had not even looked in his direction, yet he was aware by the same instinct that had at first possessed him that she knew he was present. His desire to catch her eye was becoming mingled with a certain dread, as if in a single interchange of glances the illusions of the moment would either vanish utterly or become irrevocably fixed. He forced himself, when the set was finished, to turn away, partly to avoid contact with some acquaintances who had drifted before him, and whom politeness would have obliged him to ask to dance, and partly to collect his thoughts. He determined to make a tour of the rooms and then go quietly home. Those who recognized him made way for him with passive curiosity; the middle-aged and older adding a confidential sympathy and equality that positively irritated him. For an instant he had an idea of seeking out Mrs. Tripp and claiming her as a partner, merely to show her that he danced.

He had nearly made the circuit of the room when he was surprised by the first strains of a waltz. Waltzing was not a strong feature of Indian Spring festivity, partly that the Church people had serious doubts if David's saltatory performances before the Ark included "round dances," and partly that the young had not yet mastered its difficulties. When he yielded to his impulse to look again at the dancers he found that only three or four couples had been bold enough to take the floor. Cressy McKinstry and her former partner were one of them. In his present exaltation he was not astonished to find that she had evidently picked up the art in her late visit, and was now waltzing with quiet grace and precision, but he was surprised that her partner was far from being equally perfect, and that after a few turns she stopped and smilingly disengaged her waist from his arm. As she stepped back she turned with unerring instinct to that part of the room where the master stood, and raised her eyes through the multitude of admiring faces to his. Their eyes met in an isolation as supreme as if they had been alone. It was an attraction the more dangerous because unformulated—a possession without previous pledge, promise, or even intention—a love that did not require to be "made."

He approached her quietly and even more coolly than he thought possible. "Will you allow me a trial?" he asked.

She looked in his face, and as if she had not heard the question but was following her own thought, said, "I knew you would come; I saw you when you first came in." Without another word she put her hand in his, and as if it were part of an instinctive action of drawing closer to him, caught with her advancing foot the accent of the waltz, and the next moment the room seemed to slip away from them into whirling space.

The whole thing had passed so rapidly from the moment he approached her to the first graceful swing of her full skirt at his side, that it seemed to him almost like the embrace of a lovers' meeting. He had often been as near her before, had stood at her side at school, and even leaned over her desk, but always with an irritated instinct of reserve that had equally affected her, and which he now understood. With her conscious but pale face so near his own, with the faint odor of her hair clinging to her, and with the sweet confusion of the half lingering, half withheld contact of her hand and arm, all had changed. He did not dare to reflect that he could never again approach her except with this feeling. He did not dare to think of anything; he abandoned himself to the sense that had begun with the invasion of her hair-bound myrtle in the silent school-room, and seemed to have at last led her to his arms. They were moving now in such perfect rhythm and unison that they seemed scarcely conscious of motion. Once when they neared the open window he caught a glimpse of the round moon rising above the solemn heights of the opposite shore, and felt the cool breath of mountain and river sweep his cheek and mingle a few escaped threads of her fair hair with his own. With that glimpse and that sensation the vulgarity and the tawdriness of their surroundings, the guttering candles in their sconces, the bizarre figures, the unmeaning faces seemed to be whirled far into distant space. They were alone with night and nature; it was they who were still; all else had receded in a vanishing perspective of dull reality, in which they had no part.

Play on, O waltz of Strauss! Whirl on, O love and youth! For you cannot whirl so swiftly but that this receding world will return again with narrowing circle to hem you in. Faster, O cracked clarionet! Louder, O too brazen bassoon! Keep back, O dull and earthy environment, till master and pupil have dreamed their foolish dream!

They are in fancy alone on the river-bank, only the round moon above them and their linked shadows faintly fluttering in the stream. They have drawn so closely together now that her arm is encircling his neck, her soft eyes uplifted like the moon's reflection and drowning into his; closer and closer till their hearts stop beating and their lips have met in a first kiss. Faster, O little feet! swing clear, O Cressy's skirt and keep the narrowing circle back! . . . They are again alone; the judges' dais and the emblazoning of the State caught in a single whirling flash of consciousness are changed to an altar, seen dimly through the bridal veil that covers her fair head. There is the murmur of voices mingling two lives in one. They turn and pass proudly down between the aisles of wondering festal faces. Ah! the circle is drawing closer. One more quick whirl to keep them back, O flying skirt and dainty-winged feet! Too late! The music stops. The tawdry walls shut in again, the vulgar crowds return, they stand pale and quiet, the centre of a ring of breathless admiring, frightened, or forbidding faces. Her arms fold like wings at her side. The waltz is over.

A shrill feminine chorus assail her with praises, struck here and there with a metallic ring of envy; a dozen all-daring cavaliers, made reckless by her grace and beauty, clamor for her hand in the next waltz. She replies, not to them, but to him, "Not again," and slips away in the crowd with that strange new shyness that of all her transformations seems the most delicious. Yet so conscious are they of their mutual passion that they do not miss each other, and he turns away as if their next meeting were already an appointed tryst. A few congratulate him on his skill. Johnny's paragon looks after him curiously; certain elders shake hands with him perplexedly, as if not quite sure of the professional consistency of his performance. Those charming tide-waiters on social success, the fair, artfully mingling expectation with compliment, only extract from him the laughing statement that this one waltz was the single exception allowed him from the rule of his professional conduct, and he refers them to his elder critics. A single face, loutish, looming, and vindictive, stands on among the crowd—the face of Seth Davis. He had not seen him since he left the school; he had forgotten his existence; even now he only remembered his successor, Joe Masters, and he looked curiously around to see if that later suitor of Cressy's was present. It was not until he reached the door that he began to think seriously of Seth Davis's jealous face, and was roused to a singular indignation. "Why hadn't this great fool vented his jealousy on the openly compromising Masters," he thought. He even turned and walked back with some vaguely aggressive instinct, but the young man had disappeared. With this incident still in his mind he came upon Uncle Ben and Hiram McKinstry standing among the spectators in the doorway. Why might not Uncle Ben be jealous too? and if his single waltz had really appeared so compromising why should not

Cressy's father object? But both men—albeit, McKinstry usually exhibited a vague unreasoning contempt for Uncle Ben—were unanimous in their congratulations and out-spoken admiration.

"When I see'd you sail in, Mr. Ford," said Uncle Ben, with abstract reflectiveness, "I sez to the fellers, 'lie low, boys, and you'll see style.' And when you put on them first steps, I sez, 'that's French—the latest high-toned French style—outer the best masters, and—and outer the best books. For why?' sez I. 'It's the same long, sliding stroke you see in his copies. There's that long up sweep, and that easy curve to the right with no hitch. That's the sorter swing he hez in readin' po'try too. That's why it's called the po'try of motion,' sez I. 'And you ken bet your boots, boys, it's all in the trainin' o' education.'"

"Mr. Ford," said Mr. McKinstry gravely, slightly waving a lavender-colored kid glove, with which he had elected to conceal his maimed hand, and at the same moment indicate a festal occasion: "I hev to thank ye for the way you took out that child o' mine, like ez she woz an ontried filly, and put her through her paces. I don't dance myself, partikly in that gait—which I take to be suthin' betwixt a lope and a canter and I don't get to see much dancin' nowadays on account o' bein' worried by stock, but seein' you two together just now, suthin' came over me, and I don't think I ever felt so kam in my life."

The blood rushed to the master's cheek with an unexpected consciousness of guilt and shame. "But," he stammered awkwardly, "your daughter dances beautifully herself; she has certainly had practice."

"That," said McKinstry, laying his gloved hand impressively on the master's shoulder, with the empty little finger still more emphasized by being turned backward in the net; "that may be ez it ez, but I wanted to say that it was the simple, easy, fammily touch that you gev it, that took me. Toward the end, when you kinder gathered her up and she sorter dropped her head into your breast-pocket, and seemed to go to sleep, like ez ef she was still a little girl, it so reminded me of the times when I used to tote her myself walkin' by the waggin at Platt River, that it made me wish the old woman was here to see it."

Still coloring, the master cast a rapid, sidelong glance at McKinstry's dark red face and beard, but in the slow satisfaction of his features there was no trace of that irony which the master's self-consciousness knew.

"Then your wife is not here?" said Mr. Ford abstractedly.

"She war at church. She reckoned that I'd do to look arter Cressy—she bein', so to speak, under conviction. D'ye mind walkin' this way a bit; I want to speak a word with ye?" He put his maimed hand through the master's arm, after his former fashion, and led him to a corner.

"Did ye happen to see Seth Davis about yer?"

"I believe I saw him a moment ago," returned Mr. Ford half contemptuously.

"Did he get off anythin' rough on ye?"

"Certainly not," said the master haughtily. "Why should he dare?"

"That's so," said McKinstry meditatively. "You had better keep right on in that line. That's your gait, remember. Leave him—or his father—it's the same thing—to ME. Don't YOU let yourself be roped in to this yer row betwixt me and the Davises. You ain't got no call to do it. It's already been on my mind your bringin' that gun to me in the Harrison row. The old woman hadn't oughter let you—nor Cress either. Hark to me, Mr. Ford! I reckon to stand between you and both the Davises till the cows come home—only—mind YOU give him the go-by when he happens to meander along towards you."

"I'm very much obliged to you," said Ford with disproportionately sudden choler; "but I don't propose to alter my habits for a ridiculous school-boy whom I have dismissed." The unjust and boyish petulance of his speech instantly flashed upon him, and he felt his cheek burn again.

McKinstry regarded him with dull, red, slumbrous eyes. "Don't you go to lose your best holt, Mr. Ford—and that's kam. Keep your kam—and you've allus got the dead wood on Injin Springs. I ain't got it," he continued, in his slowest, most passionless manner, "and a row more or less ain't much account to me—but YOU, you keep your kam." He paused, stepped back, and regarding the master, with a slight wave of his crippled hand over his whole person, as if indicating some personal adornment, said, "It sets you off!"

He nodded, turned, and re-entered the ball-room. Mr. Ford, without trusting himself to further speech, elbowed his way through the crowded staircase to the street. But even there his strange anger, as well as the equally strange remorse, which had seized him in McKinstry's presence, seemed to evaporate in the clear moonlight and soft summer air. There was the river-bank, with the tremulous river glancing through the dreamy mist, as they had seen it from the window together. He even turned to look back on the lighted ball-room, as if SHE might have been looking out, too. But he knew he should see her again to-morrow, and he hurriedly put aside all reserve, all thought of the future, all examination of his conduct, to walk home enwrapped in the vaguer pleasure of the past. Rupert Filgee, to whom he had never given a second thought, now peacefully slumbering beside his baby brother, had not gone home in more foolish or more dangerous company.

When he reached the hotel, he was surprised to find it only eleven o'clock. No one had returned, the building was deserted by all but the bar-keeper and a flirting chambermaid, who regarded him with aggrieved astonishment. He began to feel very foolish, and half regretted that he had not stayed to dance with Mrs. Tripp; or, at least, remained as a quiet onlooker apart from the others. With a hasty excuse about returning to write letters for the morning's post, he took a candle and slowly remounted the stairs to his room. But on entering he found himself unprepared for that singular lack of sympathy with which familiar haunts always greet our new experiences; he could hardly believe that he had left that room only two hours before; it seemed so uncongenial and strange to the sensation that was still possessing him. Yet there were his table, his books, his armchair, his bed as he had left them; even a sticky fragment of gingerbread that had fallen from Johnny's pocket. He had not yet reached that stage of absorbing passion where he was able to put the loved one in his own surroundings; she as yet had no place in this quiet room; he could scarcely think of her here, and he MUST think of her, if he had to go elsewhere. An extravagant idea of walking the street until his restless dream was over seized him, but even in his folly the lackadaisical, moonstruck quality of such a performance was too obvious. The school-house! He would go there; it was only a pleasant walk, the night was lovely, and he could bring the myrtle-spray from his desk. It was too significant now—if not too precious—to be kept there. Perhaps he had not examined it closely, nor the place where it had lain; there might be an additional sign, word, or token he had overlooked. The thought thrilled him, even while he was calmly arguing to himself that it was an instinct of caution.

The air was quieter and warmer than usual, though still characteristic of the locality in its dry, dewless clarity. The grass was yet warm from the day-long sun, and when he entered the pines that surrounded the schoolhouse, they had scarcely yet lost their spicy heat. The moon, riding high, filled the dark aisles with a delicious twilight that lent itself to his waking dreams. It was not long before to-morrow; he could easily manage to bring her here in the grove at recess, and would speak with her there. It did not occur to him what he should say, or why he should say it; it did not occur to him that he had no other provocation than her eyes, her conscious manner, her eloquent silence, and her admission that she had expected him. It did not occur to him that all this was inconsistent with what he knew of her antecedents, her character, and her habits. It was this very inconsistency that charmed and convinced him. We are always on the lookout for these miracles of passion. We may doubt the genuineness of an affection that is first-hand, but never of one that is transferred.

He approached the school-house and unlocking the door closed it behind him, not so much to keep out human intrusion as the invasion of bats and squirrels. The nearly vertical moon, while it perfectly lit the playground and openings in the pines around the house, left the interior in darkness, except the reflection upon the ceiling from the shining gravel without. Partly from a sense of precaution and partly because he was familiar with the position of the benches, he did not strike a light, and reached his own desk unerringly, drew his chair before it and unlocked it, groped in its dark recess for the myrtle spray, felt its soft silken binding with an electrical thrill, drew it out, and in the security of the darkness, raised it to his lips.

To make room for it in his breast pocket he was obliged to take out his letters—among them the well-worn one he had tried to read that morning. A mingling of pleasure and remorse came over him as he felt that it was already of the past, and as he dropped it carelessly into the empty desk it fell with a faint, hollow sound as if it were ashes to ashes.

What was that?

The noise of steps upon the gravel, light laughter, the moving of two or three shadows on the ceiling, the sound of voices, a man's, a child's, and HERS!

Could it be possible? Was not he mistaken? No! the man's voice was Masters'; the child's, Octavia's; the woman's, HERS.

He remained silent in the shadow. The school-room was not far from the trail where she would have had to pass going home from the ball. But why had she come there? had they seen him arrive? and were mischievously watching him? The sound of Cressy's voice and the lifting of the unprotected window near the door convinced him to the contrary.

"There, that'll do. Now you two can step aside. 'Tave, take him over to yon fence, and keep him there till I get in. No— thank you, sir—I can assist myself. I've done it before. It ain't the first time I've been through this window, is it, 'Tave?"

Ford's heart stopped beating. There was a moment of laughing expostulation, the sound of retreating voices, the sudden darkening of the window, the billowy sweep of a skirt, the faint quick flash of a little ankle, and Cressy

McKinstry swung herself into the room and dropped lightly on the floor.

She advanced eagerly up the moonlit passage between the two rows of benches. Suddenly she stopped; the master rose at the same moment with outstretched warning hand to check the cry of terror he felt sure would rise to her lips. But he did not know the lazy nerves of the girl before him. She uttered no outcry. And even in the faint dim light he could see only the same expression of conscious understanding come over her face that he had seen in the ball-room, mingled with a vague joy that parted her breathless lips. As he moved quickly forward their hands met; she caught his with a quick significant pressure and darted back to the window.

"Oh, 'Tave!" (very languidly.)

"Yes."

"You two had better wait for me at the edge of the trail yonder, and keep a lookout for folks going by. Don't let them see you hanging round so near. Do you hear? I'm all right."

With her hand still meaningly lifted, she stood gazing at the two figures until they slowly receded towards the distant trail. Then she turned as he approached her, the reflection of the moonlit road striking up into her shining eyes and eager waiting face. A dozen questions were upon his lips, a dozen replies were ready upon hers. But they were never uttered, for the next moment her eyes half closed, she leaned forward and fell—into a kiss.

She was the first to recover, holding his face in her hands, turned towards the moonlight, her own in passionate shadow. "Listen," she said quickly. "They think I came here to look for something I left in my desk. They thought it high fun to come with me—these two. I did come to look for something—not in my desk, but yours."

"Was it this?" he whispered, taking the myrtle from his breast. She seized it with a light cry, putting it first to her lips and then to his. Then clasping his face again between her soft palms, she turned it to the window and said: "Look at them and not at me."

He did so—seeing the two figures slowly walking in the trail. And holding her there firmly against his breast, it seemed a blasphemy to ask the question that had been upon his lips.

"That's not all," she murmured, moving his face backwards and forwards to her lips as if it were something to which she was giving breath. "When we came to the woods I felt that you would be here."

"And feeling that, you brought HIM?" said Ford, drawing back.

"Why not?" she replied indolently. "Even if he had seen you, I could have managed to have you walk home with me."

"But do you think it's quite fair? Would he like it?"

"Would HE like it?" she echoed lazily.

"Cressy," said the young man earnestly, gazing into her shadowed face. "Have you given him any right to object? Do you understand me?"

She stopped as if thinking. "Do you want me to call him in?" she said quietly, but without the least trace of archness or coquetry. "Would you rather he were here—or shall we go out now and meet him? I'll say you just came as I was going out."

What should he say? "Cressy," he asked almost curtly, "do you love me?"

It seemed such a ridiculous thing to ask, holding her thus in his arms, if it were true; it seemed such a villainous question, if it were not.

"I think I loved you when you first came," she said slowly. "It must have been that that made me engage myself to him," she added simply. "I knew I loved you, and thought only of you when I was away. I came back because I loved you. I loved you the day you came to see Maw—even when I thought you came to tell her of Masters, and to say that you couldn't take me back."

"But you don't ask me if I love you?"

"But you do—you couldn't help it now," she said confidently.

What could he do but reply as illogically with a closer embrace, albeit a slight tremor as if a cold wind had blown across the open window, passed over him. She may have felt it too, for she presently said, "Kiss me and let me go."

"But we must have a longer talk, darling—when—when—others are not waiting."

"Do you know the far barn near the boundary?" she asked.

"Yes."

"I used to take your books there, afternoons to—to—be with

you," she whispered, "and Paw gave orders that no one was to come nigh it while I was there. Come to-morrow, just before sundown."

A long embrace followed, in which all that they had not said seemed, to them at least, to become articulate on their tremulous and clinging lips. Then they separated, he unlocking the door softly to give her egress that way. She caught up a book from a desk in passing, and then slipped like a rosy shaft of the coming dawn across the fading moonlight, and a moment after her slow voice, without a tremor of excitement, was heard calling to her companions.

CHAPTER VII

The conversation which Johnny Filgee had overheard between Uncle Ben and the gorgeous stranger, although unintelligible to his infant mind, was fraught with some significance to the adult settlers of Indian Spring. The town itself, like most interior settlements, was originally a mining encampment, and as such its founders and settlers derived their possession of the soil under the mining laws that took precedence of all other titles. But although that title was held to be good even after the abandonment of their original occupation, and the establishment of shops, offices, and dwellings on the site of the deserted places, the suburbs of the town and outlying districts were more precariously held by squatters, under the presumption of their being public land open to preemption, or the settlement of school-land warrants upon them. Few of the squatters had taken the trouble to perfect even these easy titles, merely holding "possession" for agricultural or domiciliary purposes, and subject only to the invasion of "jumpers," a class of adventurers who, in the abeyance of recognized legal title, "jumped" or forcibly seized such portions of a squatter's domains as were not protected by fencing or superior force. It was therefore with some excitement that Indian Spring received the news that a Mexican grant of three square leagues, which covered the whole district, had been lately confirmed by the Government, and that action would be taken to recover possession. It was understood that it would not affect the adverse possessions held by the town under the mining laws, but it would compel the adjacent squatters like McKinstry, Davis, Masters, and Filgee, and jumpers like the Harrisons, to buy the legal title, or defend a slow but losing lawsuit. The holders of the grant—rich capitalists of San Francisco—were open to compromise to those in actual possession, and in the benefits of this compromise the unscrupulous "jumper," who had neither sown nor reaped, but simply dispossessed the squatter who had done both, shared equally with him.

A diversity of opinion as to the effect of the new claim naturally obtained; the older settlers still clung to their experiences of an easy aboriginal holding of the soil, and were sceptical both as to the validity and justice of these revived alien grants; but the newer arrivals hailed this certain tenure of legal titles as a guarantee to capital and an incentive to improvement. There was also a growing and influential party of Eastern and Northern men, who were not sorry to see a fruitful source of dissension and bloodshed removed. The feuds of the McKinstrys and Harrisons, kept alive over a boundary to which neither had any legal claim, would seem to bring them hereafter within the statute law regarding ordinary assaults without any ethical mystification. On the other hand McKinstry and Harrison would each be able to arrange any compromise with the new title holders for the lands they possessed, or make over that "actual possession" for a consideration. It was feared that both men, being naturally lawless, would unite to render any legal eviction a long and dangerous process, and that they would either be left undisturbed till the last, or would force a profitable concession. But a greater excitement followed when it was known that a section of the land had already been sold by the owners of the grant, that this section exactly covered the debatable land of the McKinstry-Harrison boundaries, and that the new landlord would at once attempt its legal possession. The inspiration of genius that had thus effected a division of the Harrison-McKinstry combination at its one weak spot excited even the admiration of the sceptics. No one in Indian Spring knew its real author, for the suit was ostensibly laid in the name of a San Francisco banker. But the intelligent reader of Johnny Filgee's late experience during the celebration will have already recognized Uncle Ben as the man, and it becomes a part of this veracious chronicle at this moment to allow him to explain, not only his intentions, but the means by which he carried them out, in his own words.

It was one afternoon at the end of his usual solitary lesson, and the master and Uncle Ben were awaiting the arrival of Rupert. Uncle Ben's educational progress lately, through dint of slow tenacity, had somewhat improved, and he had just completed from certain forms and examples in a book before him a "Letter to a Consignee" informing him that he, Uncle Ben, had just shipped "2 cwt. Ivory Elephant Tusks, 80 peculs of rice and 400bbls. prime mess pork from Indian Spring;" and another beginning "Honored Madam," and conveying in admirably artificial phraseology the "lamented decease" of the lady's husband from yellow fever, contracted on the Gold Coast, and Uncle Ben was surveying his work with critical satisfaction when the master, somewhat impatiently, consulted his watch. Uncle Ben looked up.

"I oughter told ye that Rupe didn't kalkilate to come to day."

"Indeed—why not?"

"I reckon because I told him he needn't. I allowed to—to hev a little private talk with ye, Mr. Ford, if ye didn't mind."

Mr. Ford's face did not shine with invitation. "Very well," he said, "only remember I have an engagement this afternoon."

"But that ain't until about sundown," said Uncle Ben quietly. "I won't keep ye ez long ez that."

Mr. Ford glanced quickly at Uncle Ben with a rising color. "What do you know of my engagements?" he said sharply.

"Nothin', Mr. Ford," returned Uncle Ben simply; "but hevin' bin layin' round, lookin' for ye here and at the hotel for four or five days allus about that time and not findin' you, I rather kalkilated you might hev suthin' reg'lar on hand."

There was certainly nothing in his face or manner to indicate the least evasion or deceit, or indeed anything but his usual naivete, perhaps a little perturbed and preoccupied by what he was going to say. "I had an idea of writin' you a letter," he continued, "kinder combinin' practice and confidential information, you know. To be square with you, Mr. Ford, in pint o' fact, I've got it HERE. But ez it don't seem to entirely gibe with the facts, and leaves a heap o' things onsaid and onseen, perhaps it's jest ez wall ez I read it to you myself—puttin' in a word here and there, and explainin' it gin'rally. Do you sabe?"

The master nodded, and Uncle Ben drew from his desk a rude portfolio made from the two covers of a dilapidated atlas, and took from between them a piece of blotting-paper, which through inordinate application had acquired the color and consistency of a slate, and a few pages of copy-book paper, that to the casual glance looked like sheets of exceedingly difficult music. Surveying them with a blending of chirographic pride, orthographic doubt, and the bashful consciousness of a literary amateur, he traced each line with a forefinger inked to the second joint, and slowly read aloud as follows:—

"'Mr. Ford, Teacher.

"'DEAR SIR,—Yours of the 12th rec'd and contents noted.'" ("I did'nt," explained Uncle Ben parenthetically, "receive any letter of yours, but I thought I might heave in that beginning from copy for practice. The rest is ME.") "'In refference to my having munney,'" continued Uncle Ben reading and pointing each word as he read, "'and being able to buy Ditch Stocks an' Land'"—

"One moment," said Mr. Ford interrupting, "I thought you were going to leave out copy. Come to what you have to say."

"But I HEV—this is all real now. Hold on and you'll see," said Uncle Ben. He resumed with triumphant emphasis:—

"'When it were gin'rally allowed that I haddent a red cent, I want to explain to you Mister Ford for the first time a secret. This here is how it was done. When I first came to Injian Spring, I settled down into the old Palmetto claim, near a heap of old taillings. Knowin' it were against rools, and reg'lar Chinyman's bizness to work them I diddn't let on to enyboddy what I did—witch wos to turn over some of the quarts what I thought was likely and Orrifferus. Doing this I kem uppon some pay ore which them Palmetto fellers had overlookt, or more likely had kaved in uppon them from the bank onknown. Workin' at it in od times by and large, sometimes afore sun up and sometimes after sundown, and all the time keeping up a day's work on the clame for a show to the boys, I emassed a honist fortun in 2 years of 50,000 dolers and still am. But it will be askd by the incredjulos Reeder How did you never let out anything to Injian Spring, and How did you get rid of your yeald? Mister Ford, the Anser is I took it twist a month on hoss back over to La Port and sent it by express to a bank in Sacramento, givin' the name of Daubigny, witch no one in La Port took for me. The Ditch Stok and the Land was all took in the same name, hens the secret was onreviled to the General Eye—stop a minit,'" he interrupted himself quickly as the master in an accession of impatient scepticism was about to break in upon him, "it ain't all." Then dropping his voice to a tremulous and almost funereal climax, he went on:—

"'Thus we see that pashent indurstry is Rewarded in Spite of Mining Rools and Reggylashuns, and Predgudisses agin Furrin Labor is played out and fleeth like a shad-or contenueyeth not long in One Spot, and that a Man may apear to be off no Account and yet Emass that witch is far abov rubles and Fadith not Away.

"'Hoppin' for a continneyance

"'of your fevors I remain,

"'Yours to command,

"'BENJ D'AUBIGNY.'"

The gloomy satisfaction with which Uncle Ben regarded this peroration—a satisfaction that actually appeared to be equal to the revelation itself—only corroborated the master's indignant doubts.

"Come," he said, impulsively taking the paper from Uncle Ben's reluctant hand, "how much of this is a concoction of yours and Rupe's—and how much is a true story? Do you really mean?"—

"Hold on, Mr. Ford!" interrupted Uncle Ben, suddenly fumbling in the breast-pocket of his red shirt, "I reckoned on your being a little hard with me, remembering our first talk 'bout these things—so I allowed I'd bring you some proof." Slowly extracting a long legal envelope from his pocket, he opened it, and drew out two or three crisp certificates of stock, and handed them to the master.

"Ther's one hundred shares made out to Benj Daubigny. I'd hev brought you over the deed of the land too, but ez it's rather hard to read off-hand, on account of the law palaver, I've left it up at the shanty to tackle at odd times by way of practising. But ef you like we'll go up thar, and I'll show it to you."

Still haunted by his belief in Uncle Ben's small duplicities, Mr. Ford hesitated. These were certainly bona fide certificates of stock made out to "Daubigny." But he had never actually accepted Uncle Ben's statement of his identity with that person, and now it was offered as a corroboration of a still more improbable story. He looked at Uncle Ben's simple face slightly deepening in color under his scrutiny— perhaps with conscious guilt.

"Have you made anybody your confidant? Rupe, for instance?" he asked significantly.

"In course not," replied Uncle Ben with a slight stiffening of wounded pride. "On'y yourself, Mr. Ford, and the young feller Stacey from the bank—ez was obligated to know it. In fact, I wos kalkilatin' to ask you to help me talk to him about that yer boundary land."

Mr. Ford's scepticism was at last staggered. Any practical joke or foolish complicity between the agent of the bank and a man like Uncle Ben was out of the question, and if the story were his own sole invention, he would have scarcely dared to risk so accessible and uncompromising a denial as the agent had it in his power to give.

He held out his hand to Uncle Ben. "Let me congratulate you," he said heartily, "and forgive me if your story really sounded so wonderful I couldn't quite grasp it. Now let me ask you something more. Have you had any reason for keeping this a secret, other than your fear of confessing that you violated a few bigoted and idiotic mining rules—which, after all, are binding only upon sentiment—and which your success has proved to be utterly impractical?"

"There WAS another reason, Mr. Ford," said Uncle Ben, wiping away an embarrassed smile with the back of his hand, "that is, to be square with you, WHY I thought of consultin' you. I didn't keer to have McKinstry, and"—he added hurriedly, "in course Harrison, too, know that I bought up the title to thur boundary."

"I understand," nodded the master. "I shouldn't think you would."

"Why shouldn't ye?" asked Uncle Ben quickly.

"Well—I don't suppose you care to quarrel with two passionate men."

Uncle Ben's face changed. Presently, however, with his hand to his face, he managed to manipulate another smile, only it appeared for the purpose of being as awkwardly wiped away.

"Say ONE passionate man, Mr. Ford."

"Well, one if you like," returned the master cheerfully. "But for the matter of that, why any? Come—do you mind telling me why you bought the land at all? You know it's of little value to any but McKinstry and Harrison."

"Soppose," said Uncle Ben slowly, with a great affectation of wiping his ink-spotted desk with his sleeve, "soppose that I had got kinder tired of seein' McKinstry and Harrison allus fightin' and scrimmagin' over their boundary line. Soppose I kalkilated that it warn't the sort o' thing to induce folks to settle here. Soppose I reckoned that by gettin' the real title in my hands I'd have the deadwood on both o' them, and settle the thing my own way, eh?"

"That certainly was a very laudable intention," returned Mr. Ford, observing Uncle Ben curiously, "and from what you said just now about one passionate man, I suppose you have determined already WHO to favor. I hope your public spirit will be appreciated by Indian Spring at least—if it isn't by those two men."

"You lay low and keep dark and you'll see," returned his companion with a hopefulness of speech which his some-what anxious eagerness however did not quite bear out. "But you're not goin' yet, surely," he added, as the master again absently consulted his watch. "It's on'y half past four. It's true thar ain't any more to tell," he added simply, "but I had an idea that you might hev took to this yer little story of mine more than you 'pear to be, and might be askin' questions and kinder bedevlin' me with jokes ez to what I was goin' to do— and all that. But p'raps it don't seem so wonderful to you arter all. Come to think of it—squarely now," he said, with a singular despondency, "I'm rather sick of it myself—eh?"

"My dear old boy," said Ford, grasping both his hands, with a swift revulsion of shame at his own utterly selfish abstraction, "I am overjoyed at your good luck. More than that, I can say honestly, old fellow, that it couldn't have fallen in more worthy hands, or to any one whose good fortune would have pleased me more. There! And if I've been slow and stupid in taking it in, it is because it's so wonderful, so like a fairy tale of virtue rewarded—as if you were a kind of male Cinderella, old man!" He had no intention of lying—he had no belief that he was: he had only forgotten that his previous impressions and hesitations had arisen from the very fact that he DID doubt the consistency of the story with his belief in Uncle Ben's weakness. But he thought himself now so sincere that the generous reader, who no doubt is ready to hail the perfect equity of his neighbor's good luck, will readily forgive him.

In the plenitude of this sincerity, Ford threw himself at full length on one of the long benches, and with a gesture invited Uncle Ben to make himself equally at his ease. "Come," he said with boyish gayety, "let's hear your plans, old man. To begin with, who's to share them with you? Of course there are 'the old folks at home' first; then you have brothers—and perhaps sisters?" He stopped and glanced with a smile at Uncle Ben; the idea of there being a possible female of his species struck his fancy.

Uncle Ben, who had hitherto always exercised a severe restraint—partly from respect and partly from caution—over his long limbs in the school-house, here slowly lifted one leg over another bench, and sat himself astride of it, leaning forward on his elbow, his chin resting between his hands.

"As far as the old folks goes, Mr. Ford, I'm a kind of an orphan."

"A KIND of orphan?" echoed Ford.

"Yes," said Uncle Ben, leaning heavily on his chin, so that the action of his jaws with the enunciation of each word slightly jerked his head forward as if he were imparting confidential information to the bench before him. "Yes, that is, you see, I'm all right ez far as the old man goes—HE'S dead; died way back in Mizzouri. But ez to my mother, it's sorter betwixt and between—kinder unsartain. You see, Mr. Ford, she went off with a city feller—an entire stranger to me—afore the old man died, and that's wot broke up my schoolin'. Now whether she's here, there, or yon, can't be found out, though Squire Tompkins allowed—and he were a lawyer—that the old man could get a divorce if he wanted, and that you see would make me a whole orphan, ef I keerd to prove title, ez the lawyers say. Well—thut sorter lets the old folks out. Then my brother was onc't drowned in the North Platt, and I never had any sisters. That don't leave much family for plannin' about—does it?"

"No," said the master reflectively, gazing at Uncle Ben, "unless you avail yourself of your advantages now and have one of your own. I suppose now that you are rich, you'll marry."

Uncle Ben slightly changed his position, and then with his finger and thumb began to apparently feed himself with certain crumbs which had escaped from the children's luncheon-baskets and were still lying on the bench. Intent on this occupation and without raising his eyes to the master, he returned slowly, "Well, you see, I'm sorter married already."

The master sat up quickly.

"What, YOU married—now?"

"Well, perhaps that's a question. It's a good deal like my beein' an orphan—oncertain and onsettled." He paused to pursue an evasive crumb to the end of the bench and having captured it, went on: "It was when I was younger than you be, and she warn't very old neither. But she knew a heap more than I did; and ez to readin' and writin', she was thar, I tell you, every time. You'd hev admired to see her, Mr. Ford." As he paused here as if he had exhausted the subject, the master said impatiently, "Well, where is she now?"

Uncle Ben shook his head slowly. "I ain't seen her sens I left Mizzouri, goin' on five years ago."

"But why haven't you? What was the matter?" persisted the master.

"Well—you see—I runned away. Not SHE, you know, but I—I scooted, skedaddled out here."

"But what for?" asked the master, regarding Uncle Ben with hopeless wonder. "Something must have happened. What was it? Was she"—

"She WAS a good schollard," said Uncle Ben gravely, "and allowed to be sech, by all. She stood about so high," he continued, indicating with his hand a medium height. "War little and dark complected."

"But you must have had some reason for leaving her?"

"I've sometimes had an idea," said Uncle Ben cautiously, "that mebbee runnin' away ran in some fam'lies. Now, there war my mother run off with an entire stranger, and yer's me ez run off by myself. And what makes it the more one-like is that jest as dad allus allowed he could get a devorce agin mother, so my wife could hev got one agin me for leavin' her. And it's almost an evenhanded game that she hez. It's there where the oncertainty comes in."

"But are you satisfied to remain in this doubt? or do you propose, now that you are able, to institute a thorough search for her?"

"I was kalkilatin' to look around a little," said Uncle

Ben simply.

"And return to her if you find her?" continued the master.

"I didn't say that, Mr. Ford."

"But if she hasn't got a divorce from you that's what you'll have to do, and what you ought to do—if I understand your story. For by your own showing, a more causeless, heartless, and utterly inexcusable desertion than yours, I never heard of."

"Do you think so?" said Uncle Ben with exasperating simplicity.

"Do I think so?" repeated Mr. Ford, indignantly. "Everybody'll think so. They can't think otherwise. You say you deserted her, and you admit she did nothing to provoke it."

"No," returned Uncle Ben quickly, "nothin'. Did I tell you, Mr. Ford, that she could play the pianner and sing?"

"No," said Mr. Ford, curtly, rising impatiently and crossing the room. He was more than half convinced that Uncle Ben was deceiving him. Either under the veil of his hide-bound simplicity he was an utterly selfish, heartless, secretive man, or else he was telling an idiotic falsehood.

"I'm sorry I can neither congratulate you nor condole with you on what you have just told me. I cannot see that you have the least excuse for delaying a single moment to search for your wife and make amends for your conduct. And if you want my opinion it strikes me as being a much more honorable way of employing your new riches than mediating in your neighbors' squabbles. But it's getting late and I'm afraid we must bring our talk to an end. I hope you'll think this over before we meet again—and think differently."

Nevertheless, as they both left the schoolhouse, Mr. Ford lingered over the locking of the door to give Uncle Ben a final chance for further explanation. But none came. The new capitalist of Indian Spring regarded him with an intensification of his usual half sad, half embarrassed smile, and only said: "You understand this yer's a secret, Mr. Ford?"

"Certainly," said Ford with ill-concealed irritation.

"'Bout my bein' sorter married?"

"Don't be alarmed," he responded dryly; "it's not a taking story."

They separated; Uncle Ben, more than ever involved in his usual unsatisfactory purposes, wending his way towards his riches; the master lingering to observe his departure before he plunged, in virtuous superiority, into the woods that fringed the Harrison and McKinstry boundaries.

CHAPTER VIII

The religious attitude which Mrs. McKinstry had assumed towards her husband's weak civilized tendencies was not entirely free from human rancor. That strong loyal nature which had unsexed itself in the one idea of duty, now that duty seemed to be no longer appreciated took refuge in her forgotten womanhood and in the infinitesimally small arguments, resources, and manoeuvres at its command. She had conceived a singular jealousy of this daughter who had changed her husband's nature, and who had supplanted the traditions of the household life; she had acquired an exaggerated depreciation of those feminine charms which had never been a factor in her own domestic happiness. She saw in her husband's desire to mitigate the savage austerities of their habits only a weak concession to the powers of beauty and adornment—degrading vanities she had never known in their life-long struggle for frontier supremacy—that had never brought them victorious out of that struggle. "Frizzles," "furblows," and "fancy fixin's" had never helped them in their exodus across the plains; had never taken the place of swift eyes, quick ears, strong hands, and endurance; had never nursed the sick or bandaged the wounded. When envy or jealousy invades the female heart after forty it is apt to bring a bitterness which knows no attenuating compensation in that coquetry, emulation, passionate appeal, or innocent tenderness, which makes tolerable the jealous caprices of the younger woman. The struggle for rivalry is felt to be hopeless, the power of imitation is gone. Of her forgotten womanhood Mrs. McKinstry revived only a capacity to suffer meanly and inflict mean suffering upon others. In the ruined castle of her youth, and the falling in of banqueting hall and bower, the dungeon and torture-chamber appeared to have been left, or, to use her own metaphor, she had querulously complained to the parson that, "Accordin' to some folks, she mout hev bin the barren fig-tree e-lected to bear persimmums."

Her methods were not entirely different from those employed by her suffering sisterhood in like emergencies. The unlucky Hiram, "worrited by stock," was hardly placated or consoled by learning from her that it was only the result of his own weakness, acting upon the 'cussedness of the stock-dispersing Harrisons; the perplexity into which he was thrown by the news of the new legal claim to his land was not soothed by the suggestion that it was a trick of that Yankee civilization to which he was meanly succumbing. She who had always been a rough but devoted nurse in sickness was now herself overtaken by vague irregular disorders which involved the greatest care and the absence of all exciting causes. The attendance of McKinstry and Cressy at a "crazy quilting party" had brought on "blind chills;" the importation of a melodeon for Cressy to play on had superinduced an "innerd rash," and a threatened attack of "palsy creeps" had only been warded off by the timely postponement of an evening party suggested by her daughter. The old nomadic instinct, morbidly excited by her discontent, caused her to lay artful plans for a further emigration. She knew she had the germs of "mash fever" caught from the adjacent river; she related mysterious information, gathered in "class meeting," of the superior facilities for stock raising on the higher foot-hills; she resuscitated her dead and gone Missouri relations in her daily speech, to a manifest invidious comparison with the living; she revived even the incidents of her early married life with the same baleful intent. The acquisition of a few "biled shirts" by Hiram for festive appearances with Cressy painfully reminded her that he had married her in "hickory;" she further accented the change by herself appearing in her oldest clothes, on the hypothesis that it was necessary for some one to keep up the traditions of the past.

Her attitude towards Cressy would have been more decided had she ever possessed the slightest influence over her, or had even understood her with the intuitive sympathies of the maternal relations. Yet she went so far as to even openly regret the breaking off of the match with Seth Davis, whose family, at least, still retained the habits and traditions she revered; but she was promptly silenced by her husband informing her that words "that had to be tuk back" had already passed between him and Seth's father, and that, according to those same traditions, blood was more likely to be spilled than mingled. Whether she was only withheld from attempting a reconciliation herself through lack of tact and opportunity remains to be seen. For the present she encouraged Masters's attentions under a new and vague idea that a flirtation which distracted Cressy from her studies was displeasing to McKinstry and inimical to his plans. Blindly ignorant of Mr. Ford's possible relations to her daughter, and suspecting nothing, she felt towards him only a dull aversion as being the senseless pivot of her troubles. Seeing no one, and habitually closing her ears to any family allusion to Cressy's social triumphs, she was unaware of even the popular admiration their memorable waltz had excited.

On the morning of the day that Uncle Ben had confided to the master his ingenious plan for settling the boundary disputes, the barking of McKinstry's yellow dog announced the approach of a stranger to the ranch. It proved to be Mr.

Stacey—not only as dazzlingly arrayed as when he first rose above Johnny Filgee's horizon, but wearing, in addition to his jaunty business air, a look of complacent expectation of the pretty girl whom he had met at the ball. He had not seen her for a month. It was a happy inspiration of his own that enabled him to present himself that morning in the twin functions of a victorious Mercury and Apollo.

McKinstry had to be summoned from an adjacent meadow, while Cressy, in the mean time, undertook to entertain the gallant stranger. This was easily done. It was part of her fascinations that, disdaining the ordinary real or assumed ignorance of the ingenue of her class, she generally exhibited to her admirers (with perhaps the single exception of the master) a laughing consciousness of the state of mind into which her charms had thrown them. She understood their passion if she could not accept it. This to a bashful rustic community was helpful, but in the main unsatisfactory; with advances so promptly unmasked, the most strategic retreat was apt to become an utter rout. Leaning against the lintel of the door, her curved hand shading the sparkling depths of her eyes, and the sunlight striking down upon the pretty curves of her languid figure, she awaited the attack.

"I haven't seen you, Miss Cressy, since we danced together—a month ago."

"That was mighty rough papers," said Cressy, who was purposely dialectical to strangers, "considering that you trapsed up and down the lane, past the house, twice yesterday."

"Then you saw me?" said the young man, with a slightly discomfited laugh.

"I did. And so did the hound, and so, I reckon, did Joe

Masters and the hired man. And when you pranced back on the home stretch, there was the hound, Masters, the hired man, and Maw all on your trail, and Paw bringin' up the rear with a shot-gun. There was about a half a mile of you altogether." She removed her hand from her eyes to indicate with a lazily graceful sweep this somewhat imaginative procession, and laughed.

"You are certainly well guarded," said Stacey hesitatingly; "and looking at you, Miss Cressy," he added boldly, "I don't wonder at it."

"Well, it IS reckoned that next to Paw's boundaries I'm pretty well protected from squatters and jumpers."

Forceful and quaint as her language was, the lazy sweetness of her intonation, and the delicate refinement of her face, more than atoned for it. It was unconventional and picturesque as her gestures. So at least thought Mr. Stacey, and it emboldened him to further gallantry.

"Well, Miss Cressy, as my business with your father to-day was to try to effect a compromise of his boundary claims, perhaps you might accept my services in your own behalf."

"Which means," responded the young lady pertly, "the same thing to ME as to Paw. No trespassers but yourself. Thank you, sir." She twirled lightly on her heel and dropped him that exaggerated curtsey known to the school-children as a "cheese." It permitted in its progress the glimpse of a pretty little slipper which completed his subjugation.

"Well, if it's only a fair compromise," he began laughingly.

"Compromise means somebody giving up. Who is it?" she asked.

The infatuated Stacey had reached the point of thinking this repartee if possible more killing than his own.

"Ha! That's for Miss Cressy to say."

But the young lady leaning back against the lintel with the comfortable ease of being irresponsibly diverted, sagely pointed out that that was the function of the arbitrator.

"Ah well, suppose we begin by giving up Seth Davis, eh? You see that I'm pretty well posted, Miss Cressy."

"You alarm me," said Cressy sweetly. "But I reckon he HAD given up."

"He was in the running that night at the ball. Looked half savage while I was dancing with you. Wanted to eat me."

"Poor Seth! And he used to be SO particular in his food," said the witty Cressy.

Mr. Stacey was convulsed. "And there's Mr. Dabney—Uncle Ben," he continued, "eh? Very quiet but very sly. A dark horse, eh? Pretends to take lessons for the sake of being near some one, eh? Would he were a boy again because somebody else is a girl?"

"I should be frightened of you if you lived here always," returned Cressy with invincible naivete; "but perhaps then you wouldn't know so much."

Stacey simply accepted this as a compliment. "And there's Masters," he said insinuatingly.

"Not Joe?" said Cressy with a low laugh, turning her eyes to the door.

"Yes," said Stacey with a quick, uneasy smile. "Ah! I see we mustn't drop HIM. Is he out THERE?" he added, trying to follow the direction of her eyes.

But the young girl kept her face studiously averted. "Is that all?" she asked after a pause.

"Well—there's that solemn school-master, who cut me out of the waltz with you—that Mr. Ford."

Had he been a perfectly cool and impartial observer he would have seen the slight tremor cross Cressy's soft eyelids even in profile, followed by that momentary arrest of her whole face, mouth, dimples, and eyes, which had overtaken it the night the master entered the ball-room. But he was neither, and it passed quickly and unnoticed. Her usual lithe but languid play of expression and color came back, and she turned her head lazily towards the speaker. "There's Paw coming. I suppose you wouldn't mind giving me a sample of your style of arbitrating with him, before you try it on me?"

"Certainly not," said Stacey, by no means displeased at the prospect of having so pretty and intelligent a witness in the daughter of what he believed would form an attractive display of his diplomatic skill and graciousness to the father. "Don't go away. I've got nothing to say Miss Cressy could not understand and answer."

The jingling of spurs, and the shadow of McKinstry and his shot-gun falling at this moment between the speaker and Cressy, spared her the necessity of a reply. McKinstry cast an uneasy glance around the apartment, and not seeing Mrs. McKinstry looked relieved, and even the deep traces of the loss of a valuable steer that morning partly faded from his Indian-red complexion. He placed his shot-gun carefully in the corner, took his soft felt hat from his head, folded it and put it in one of the capacious pockets of his jacket, turned to his daughter, and laying his maimed hand familiarly on her shoulder, said gravely, without looking at Stacey, "What might the stranger be wantin', Cress?"

"Perhaps I'd better answer that myself," said Stacey briskly. "I'm acting for Benham and Co., of San Francisco, who have bought the Spanish title to part of this property. I"—

"Stop there!" said McKinstry, in a voice dull but distinct. He took his hat from his pocket, put it on, walked to the corner and took up his gun, looked at Stacey for the first time with narcotic eyes that seemed to drowsily absorb his slight figure, then put the gun back half contemptuously, and with a wave of his hand towards the door, said: "We'll settle this yer outside. Cress, you stop in here. There's man's talk goin' on."

"But, Paw," said Cressy, laying her hand languidly on her father's sleeve without the least change of color or amused expression. "This gentleman has come over here on a compromise."

"On a—WHICH?" said McKinstry, glancing scornfully out of the door for some rare species of mustang vaguely suggested to him in that unfamiliar word.

"To see if we couldn't come to some fair settlement," said Stacey. "I've no objection to going outside with you, but I think we can discuss this matter here just as well." His fine feathers had not made him a coward, although his heart had beaten a little faster at this sudden recollection of the dangerous reputation of his host.

"Go on," said McKinstry.

"The plain facts of the case are these," continued Stacey, with more confidence. "We have sold a strip of this property covering the land in dispute between you and Harrison. We are bound to put our purchaser in peaceable possession. Now to save time we are willing to buy that possession of any man who can give it. We are told that you can."

"Well, considerin' that for the last four years I've been fightin' night and day agin them low-down Harrisons for it, I reckon you've been lied to," said McKinstry deliberately. "Why—except the clearing on the north side, whar I put up a barn, thar ain't an acre of it as hasn't been shifted first this side and then that as fast ez I druv boundary stakes and fences, and the Harrisons pulled 'em up agin. Thar ain't more than fifty acres ez I've hed a clear hold on, and I wouldn't hev had that ef it hadn't bin for the barn, the raisin' alone o' which cost me a man, two horses, and this yer little finger."

"Put us in possession of even that fifty acres, and WE'LL undertake to hold the rest and eject those Harrisons from it," returned Stacey complacently. "You understand that the moment we've made a peaceable entrance to even a foothold on your side, the Harrisons are only trespassers, and with the title to back us we can call on the whole sheriff's posse to put them off. That's the law."

"That ar the law?" repeated McKinstry meditatively.

"Yes," said Stacey. "So," he continued, with a self-satisfied smile to Cressy, "far from being hard on you, Mr. McKinstry, we're rather inclined to put you on velvet. We offer you a fair price for the only thing you can give us— actual possession; and we help you with your old grudge against the Harrisons. We not only clear them out, but we pay YOU for even the part they held adversely to you."

Mr. McKinstry passed his three whole fingers over his forehead and eyes as if troubled by a drowsy aching. "Then you don't reckon to hev anythin' to say to them Harrisons?"

"We don't propose to recognize them in the matter at all," returned Stacey.

"Nor allow 'em anythin'?"

"Not a cent! So you see, Mr. McKinstry," he continued magnanimously, yet with a mischievous smile to Cressy, "there is nothing in this amicable discussion that requires to be settled outside."

"Ain't there?" said McKinstry, in a dull, deliberate voice, raising his eyes for the second time to Stacey. They were bloodshot, with a heavy, hanging furtiveness, not unlike one of his own hunted steers. "But I ain't kam enuff in yer." He moved to the door with a beckoning of his fateful hand. "Outside a minit—EF you please."

Stacey started, shrugged his shoulders, and half defiantly stepped beyond the threshold. Cressy, unchanged in color or expression, lazily followed to the door.

"Wot," said McKinstry, slowly facing Stacey; "wot ef I refoose? Wot ef I say I don't allow any man, or any bank, or any compromise, to take up my quo'r'lls? Wot ef I say that low-down and mean as them Harrisons is, they don't begin to be ez mean, ez low-down, ez underhanded, ez sneakin' ez that yer compromise? Wot ef I say that ef that's the kind o' hogwash that law and snivelization offers me for peace and quietness, I'll take the fightin', and the law-breakin', and the sheriff, and all h-ll for his posse instead? Wot ef I say that?"

"It will only be my duty to repeat it," said Stacey, with an affected carelessness which, however, did not conceal his surprise and his discomfiture. "It's no affair of mine."

"Unless," said Cressy, assuming her old position against the lintel of the door, and smoothing the worn bear-skin that served as a mat with the toe of her slipper, "unless you've mixed it up with your other arbitration, you know."

"Wot other arbitration?" asked McKinstry suddenly, with murky eyes.

Stacey cast a rapid, half indignant glance at the young girl, who received it with her hands tucked behind her back, her lovely head bent submissively forward, and a prolonged little laugh.

"Oh nothing, Paw," she said, "only a little private foolishness betwixt me and the gentleman. You'd admire to hear him talk, Paw—about other things than business. He's just that chipper and gay."

Nevertheless, as with a muttered "Good-morning" the young fellow turned away, she quietly brushed past her father, and followed him—with her hands still penitently behind her, and the rosy palms turned upward—as far as the gate. Her single long Marguerite braid of hair trailing down her back nearly to the hem of her skirt, appeared to accent her demure reserve. At the gate she shaded her eyes with her hand, and glanced upward.

"It don't seem to be a good day for arbitrating. A trifle early in the season, ain't it?"

"Good-morning, Miss McKinstry."

She held out her hand. He took it with an affected ease but

cautiously, as if it had been the velvet paw of a young panther who had scratched him. After all, what was she but the cub of the untamed beast, McKinstry? He was well out of it! He was not revengeful—but business was business, and he had given them the first chance.

As his figure disappeared behind the buckeyes of the lane, Cressy cast a glance at the declining sun. She re-entered the house, and went directly to her room. As she passed the window, she could see her father already remounted galloping towards the tules, as if in search of that riparian "kam" his late interview had disturbed. A few straggling bits of color in the sloping meadows were the children coming home from school. She hastily tied a girlish sun-bonnet under her chin, and slipping out of the back door, swept like a lissom shadow along the line of fence until she seemed to melt into the umbrage of the woods that fringed the distant north boundary.

CHAPTER IX

Meanwhile, unaware of her husband's sudden relapse to her old border principles and of the visit that had induced it, Mrs. McKinstry was slowly returning from a lugubrious recital of her moods and feelings at the parson's. As she crossed the barren flat and reached the wooded upland midway between the school-house and the ranch, she saw before her the old familiar figure of Seth Davis lounging on the trail. In her habitual loyalty to her husband's feuds she would probably have stalked defiantly past him, notwithstanding her late regrets of the broken engagement, but Seth began to advance awkwardly towards her. In fact, he had noticed the tall, gaunt, plaid-shawled and holland-bonneted figure approaching, and had waited for it.

As he seemed intent upon getting in her way she stopped and raised her right hand warningly before her. In spite of the shawl and the sun-bonnet, suffering had implanted a rude Runic dignity to her attitude. "Words that hev to be took back, Seth Davis," she said hastily, "hev passed between you and my man. Out of my way, then, that I may pass, too."

"Not much betwixt you and me, Aunt Rachel," he said with slouching deprecation, using the old household title by which he had familiarly known her. "I've nothin agin you—and I kin prove it by wot I'm yer to say. And I ain't trucklin' to yer for myself, for ez far ez me and your'n ez concerned," he continued, with a malevolent glance, "thar ain't gold enough in Caleforny to mak the weddin' ring that could hitch me and Cress together. I want to tell you that you're bein' played; that you're bein' befooled and bamboozled and honey-fogled. Thet while you're groanin' at class-meetin' and Hiram's quo'llin' with Dad, and Joe Masters waitin' round to pick up any bone that's throwed him, that sneakin', hypocritical Yankee school-master is draggin' your daughter to h-ll with him on the sly."

"Quit that, Seth Davis," said Mrs. McKinstry sternly, "or be man enough to tell it to a man. That's Hiram's business to know."

"And what if he knows it well enough and winks at it? What if he's willin' enough to truckle to it, to curry favor with them sneakin' Yanks?" said Seth malignantly.

A spasm of savage conviction seized Mrs. McKinstry. But it was more from her jealous fears of her husband's disloyalty than concern for her daughter's transgression. Nevertheless, she said desperately, "It's a lie. Where are your proofs?"

"Proofs?" returned Seth. "Who is it sneaks around the school-house to have private talks with the school-master, and edges him on with Cressy afore folks? Your husband. Who goes sneakin' off every arternoon with that same cantin' hound of a school-master? Your daughter. Who's been carryin' on together, and hidin' thick enough to be ridden out on a rail together? Your daughter and the school-master. Proofs?—ask anybody. Ask the children. Look yar—you, Johnny—come here."

He had suddenly directed his voice to a blackberry bush near the trail, from which the curly head of Johnny Filgee had just appeared. That home-returning infant painfully disengaged himself, his slate, his books, and his small dinner-pail half filled with fruit as immature as himself, and came towards them sideways.

"Yer's a dime, Johnny, to git some candy," said Seth, endeavoring to distort his passion-set face into a smile.

Johnny Filgee's small, berry-stained palm promptly closed over the coin.

"Now, don't lie. Where's Cressy?"

"Kithin' her bo."

"Good boy. What bo?"

Johnny hesitated. He had once seen the school-master and Cressy together; he had heard it whispered by the other children that they loved each other. But looking at Seth and Mrs. McKinstry he felt that something more tremendous than this stupid fact was required of him for grown-up people, and being honest and imaginative, he determined that it should be worth the money.

"Speak up, Johnny, don't be afeard to tell."

Johnny was not "afeard"—he was only thinking. He had it! He remembered that he had just seen his paragon, the brilliant Stacey, coming from the boundary woods. What more poetical and startlingly effective than to connect him with Cressy? He replied promptly:—

"Mithter Thtathy. He gave her a watch and ring of truly gold. Goin' to be married at Thacramento."

"You lyin' limb," said Seth, seizing him roughly. But Mrs. McKinstry interposed.

"Let that brat go," she said with gleaming eyes. "I want to talk to you." Seth released Johnny. "It's a trick," he said, "he's bin put up to it by that Ford."

But Johnny, after securing a safe vantage behind the blackberry bush, determined to give them another trial—with facts.

"I know mor'n that," he called out.

"Git—you measly pup," said Seth savagely.

"I know Theriff Briggth, he rid over the boundary with a lot o' men and horthes," said Johnny, with that hurried delivery with which he was able to estop interruption. "Theed 'em go by. Maur Harrithon theth his dad's goin' to chuck out ole McKinthtry. Hooray!"

Mrs. McKinstry turned her dark face sharply on Seth. "What's that he sez?"

"Nothin' but children's gassin'," he answered, meeting her eyes with an evil consciousness half loutish, half defiant, "and ef it war true, it would only sarve Hiram McKinstry right."

She laid her hand upon his shoulder with swift suspicion. "Out o' my way, Seth Davis," she said suddenly, pushing him aside. "Ef this ez any underhanded work of yours, you'll pay for it."

She strode past him in the direction of Johnny, but at the approach of the tall woman with the angry eyes, the boy flew. She hesitated a moment, turned again with a threatening wave of the hand to Seth, and started off rapidly in the direction of the boundary.

She had not placed so much faith in the boy's story as in the vague revelation of evil in Davis's manner. If there was any "cussedness" afoot, Seth, convinced of Cressy's unfaithfulness, and with no further hope of any mediation from the parents, would know it. Unless Hiram had been warned, he was still lulled in his fatuous dream of civilization. At that time he and his men were in the tules with the stock; to be satisfied, she herself must go to the boundary.

She reached the ridge of the cottonwoods and sycamores, and a few hundred yards further brought her to the edge of that gentle southern slope which at last sank into the broad meadow of the debatable ground. In spite of Stacey's invidious criticism of its intrinsic value, this theatre of savage dissension, violence, and bloodshed was by some irony of nature a pastoral landscape of singular and peaceful repose. The soft glacis stretching before her was in spring cerulean with lupins, and later starred with mariposas. The meadow was transversely crossed by a curving line of alders that indicated a rare water-course, of which in the dry season only a single pool remained to flash back the unvarying sky. There had been no attempt at cultivation of this broad expanse; wild oats, mustard, and rank grasses left it a tossing sea of turbulent and variegated color whose waves rode high enough to engulf horse and rider in their choking depths. Even the traces of human struggle, the uprooted stakes, scattered fence-rails, and empty post-holes were forever hidden under these billows of verdure. Midway of the field and near the water-course arose McKinstry's barn—the solitary human structure whose rude, misshapen, bulging sides and swallow-haunted eaves bursting with hay from the neighboring pasture, seemed however only an extravagant growth of the prolific soil. Mrs. McKinstry gazed at it anxiously. There was no sign of life or movement near or around it; it stood as it had always stood, deserted and solitary. But turning her eyes to the right, beyond the water-course, she could see a slight regular undulation of the grassy sea and what appeared to be the drifting on its surface of half a dozen slouched hats in the direction of the alders. There was no longer any doubt; a party from the other side was approaching the border.

A shout and the quick galloping of hoofs behind her sent a thrill of relief to her heart. She had barely time to draw aside as her husband and his followers swept past her down the slope. But it needed not his furious cry, "The Harrisons hev sold us out," to tell her that the crisis had come.

She held her breath as the cavalcade diverged, and in open order furiously approached the water-course, and she could see a sudden check and hesitation in the movement in the meadow at that unlooked-for onset. Then she thought of the barn. It would be a rallying-point for them if driven back—a tower of defence if besieged. There were arms secreted beneath the hay for such an emergency. She would run there, swing-to its open doors, and get ready to barricade them.

She ran crouchingly, seeking the higher grasses and brambles of the ridge to escape observation from the meadow until she could descend upon the barn from the rear. She threw aside her impeding shawl; her brown holland sun-bonnet, torn off her head and hanging by its strings from her shoulders, let her coarse silver-threaded hair stream like a mane over her back; her face and hands were bleeding from thorns and whitened by dust. But she struggled on fiercely like some hunted animal until she reached the descending trail, when, letting herself go blindly, only withheld by the long grasses she clutched at wildly on either side, she half fell, half stumbled down the slope and emerged beside the barn, breathless and exhausted.

But what a contrast was there! For an instant she could scarcely believe that she had left the ridge with her husband's savage outcry in her ears, and in her eyes the swift vision of his furious cavalcade. The boundary meadow was hidden by the soft lines of graceful willows in whose dim recesses the figures of the passionate horsemen seemed to have melted forever. There was nothing now to interrupt the long vista of peaceful beauty that stretched before her through this lonely hollow to the distant sleeping hills. The bursting barn in the foreground, heaped with grain that fringed its eaves and bristled from its windows and doors until its unlovely bulk was hidden in trailing feathery outlines; the gentle flutter of wings and soothing twitter of swallows and jays around its open rafters, and the drifting shadows of a few circling crows above it; the drowsy song of bees on the wild mustard that half hid its walls with yellow bloom; the sound of faintly-trickling water in one of those old Indian-haunted springs that had given its name to the locality; all these for an instant touched the senses of this hard, fierce woman as she had not been touched since she was a girl. For one brief moment the joys of peace and that matured repose that never had been hers flashed upon her; but with it came the savage consciousness that even now it was being wrested away, and the thought fired her blood again. She listened eagerly for a second in the direction of the meadow; there was no report of fire-arms—there was yet time to prepare the barn for defence. She ran to the front of the building and seized the latch of the half-closed door. A little feminine cry that was half a laugh came from within, with the rapid rustle of a skirt and as the door swung open a light figure vanished through the rear window. The slanting sunlight falling in the shadowed interior disclosed only the single erect figure of the school-master John Ford.

The first confusion and embarrassment of an interrupted rendezvous that had colored Ford's cheeks, gave way to a look of alarm as he caught sight of the bleeding face and dishevelled figure of Mrs. McKinstry. She saw it. To her distorted fancy it seemed only a proof of deeper guilt. Without a word she closed the heavy door behind her and swung the huge cross-bar unaided to its place. She then turned and confronted him, wiping the dust from her face and arms with her torn and dangling sun-bonnet in a way that recalled her attitude on the first day he had met her.

"That was Cress with ye?" she said.

He hesitated, still gazing at her in wonder.

"Don't lie."

He started. "I don't propose to," he retorted indignantly. "It was"—

"I don't ask ye how long this yer's bin goin' on," she said, pointing to Cressy's sun-bonnet, a few books, and a scattered nosegay of wild flowers lying on the hay; "and I don't want to know. In five minutes either her father will be here, or them hell-hounds of Harrison's who've sold him out will swarm round this barn to git possesshun. Ef this yer"—she again pointed contemptuously to the objects just indicated— "means that you've cast your lot with US and kalkilate to take our bitter with our sweet, ye'll lift up that stack of hay and bring out a gun to help defend it. Ef you're meanin' anythin' else, Ford, you'll hide yourself in that hay till Hiram comes and has time enough to attend to ye."

"And if I choose to do neither?" he said haughtily.

She looked at him in unutterable scorn. "There's the

winder—take it while there's time, afore I bar it. Ef you see Hiram, tell him ye left an old woman behind ye to defend the place whar you uster hide with her darter."

Before he could reply there was a distant report, followed almost directly by another. With a movement of irritation he walked to the window, turned and looked at her—bolted it, and came back.

"Where's that gun?" he said almost rudely.

"I reckon's that would fetch ye," she said, dragging away the hay and disclosing a long trough-like box covered with tarpaulin. It proved to contain powder, shot, and two guns. He took one.

"I suppose I may know what I am fighting for?" he said dryly.

"Ye might say 'Cress' ef they"—indicating the direction of the reports—"happen to ask ye," she returned with equal sobriety. "Jess now ye kin take your stand up thar in the loft and see what's comin'."

He did not linger, but climbed to the place assigned him, glad to escape the company of the woman who at that moment he almost hated. In his unreflecting passion for Cressy he had always evaded the thought of this relationship or propinquity; the mother had recalled it to him in a way that imperilled even his passion for the daughter; his mind was wholly preoccupied with the idiotic, exasperating, and utterly hopeless position that had been forced upon him. In the bitterness of his spirit his sense of personal danger was so far absorbed that he speculated on the chance bullet in the melee that might end his folly and relieve him of responsibility. Shut up in a barn with a furious woman, in a lawless defence of questionable rights—with the added conscious-ness that an equally questionable passion had drawn him into it, and that SHE knew it—death seemed to offer the only escape from the explanation he could never give. If another sting could have been added it was the absurd conviction that Cressy would not appreciate his sacrifice, but was perhaps even at that moment calmly congratulating herself on the felicitousness of the complication in which she had left him.

Suddenly he heard a shout and the tramping of horse. The sides of the loft were scantily boarded to allow the extension of the pent-up grain, and between the interstices Ford, without being himself seen, had an uninterrupted view of the plain between him and the line of willows. As he gazed, five men hurriedly issued from the extreme left and ran towards the barn. McKinstry and his followers simultaneously broke from the same covert further to the right and galloped forward to intercept them. But although mounted, the greater distance they had to traverse brought them to the rear of the building only as the Harrison party came to a sudden halt before the closed and barricaded doors of the usually defenceless barn. The discomfiture of the latter was greeted by a derisive shout from the McKinstry party—albeit, equally astonished. But in that brief moment Ford recognized in the leader of the Harrisons the well-known figure of the Sheriff of Tuolumne. It needed only this to cap the climax of the fatality that seemed to pursue him. He was no longer a lawless opposer of equally lawless forces, but he was actually resisting the law itself. He understood the situation now. It was some idiotic blunder of Uncle Ben's that had precipitated this attack.

The belligerents had already cocked their weapons, although the barn was still a rampart between the parties. But an adroit flanker of McKinstry's, creeping through the tall mustard, managed to take up an enfilading position as the Harrisons advanced to break in the door. A threatening shout from the ambuscaded partisans caused them to hurriedly fall back towards the rear of the barn. There was a pause, and then began the usual Homeric chaff,—with this Western difference that it was cunningly intended to draw the other's fire.

"Why don't you blaze away at the door, you— —! It won't hurt ye!"

"He's afraid the bolt will shoot back!" Laughter from the McKinstrys.

"Come outer the tall grass and show yourself, you black, mud-eating gopher."

"He can't. He's dropped his grit and is sarchin' for it." Goading laughter from the Harrisons.

Each man waited for that single shot which would precipitate the fight. Even in their lawlessness the rude instinct of the duello swayed them. The officer of the law recognized the principle as well as its practical advantage in a collision, but he hesitated to sacrifice one of his men in an attack on the barn, which would draw the fire of McKinstry at that necessarily fatal range. As a brave man he would have taken the risk himself, but as a prudent one, he reflected that his hurriedly collected posse were all partisans, and if he fell the conflict would resolve itself into a purely partisan struggle without a single unprejudiced witness to justify his conduct in the popular eye. The master also knew this; it had checked his first impulse to come forward as a mediator; his only reliance now was on Mrs. McKinstry's restraint and the sheriff's forbearance. The next instant both seemed to be imperilled.

"Well, why don't you wade in?" sneered Dick McKinstry; "who do you reckon's hidden in the barn?"

"I'll tell ye," said a harsh, passionate voice from the hill-side. "It's Cressy McKinstry and the school-master hidin' in the hay."

Both parties turned quickly towards the intruder who had approached them unperceived. But the speech was followed by a more startling revulsion of sentiment as Mrs. McKinstry's voice rang out from the barn, "You lie, Seth Davis!"

The brief advantage offered to the sheriff in Davis's advent as a neutral witness, was utterly lost by this unlooked-for revelation of Mrs. McKinstry's presence in the barn! The fates were clearly against him! A woman in the fight, and an old one at that! A white woman to be forcibly ejected! In the whole unwritten code of Southwestern chivalry there was no such precedent.

"Stand back," he said disgustedly to his followers, "stand back and let the d—d barn slide. But you, Hiram McKinstry, I'll give YOU five minutes to shake yourself clear of your wife's petticoats and git!" His blood was up now—the quicker from his momentary weakness and the trick of which he thought himself a dupe.

Again the fatal signal seemed imminent, again it was delayed. For Hiram McKinstry, with clanking spurs and rifle in hand stepped from behind the barn, full in the presence of his antagonists.

"Ez to my gitten in five minits," he began in his laziest, drowsiest manner, "we'll see when the time's up. But jest now words hev passed betwixt my wife and Seth Davis.

Afore anythin' else goes on yer, he's got to take HIS back. My wife allows he lies; I allow he lies too, and I stan' here to say it."

The right of personal insult to precedence of redress was too old a frontier principle to be gainsaid now. Both parties held back and every eye was turned to where Seth Davis had been standing. But he had disappeared.

Where?

When Mrs. McKinstry hurled her denial from the barn, he had taken advantage of the greater surprise to leap to one of the trusses of hay that projected beyond the loft, and secure a footing from which he quickly scrambled through the open scantling to the interior. The master who, startled by his voice, had made his way through the loose grain to the rear, reached it as Seth half crawled, half tumbled through. Their eyes met in a single flash of rage, but before Seth could utter an outcry, the master had dropped his gun, seized him around the neck and crammed a thick handful of the soft hay he had hurriedly snatched up into his face and gasping mouth. A furious but silent struggle ensued; the yielding hay on which they both fell deadened all sound of a scuffle and concealed them from view; masses of it, already loosened by the intruder's entrance, and dislodged in their contortions began to slip through the opening to the ground. The master, still uppermost and holding Seth firmly down, allowed himself to slip with them, shoving his adversary before him; the maddened Missourian detecting his purpose, made a desperate attempt to change his position, and succeeded in raising his knee against the master's chest. Ford, guarding against what seemed to be only a wrestler's strategy, contented himself by locking the bent knee firmly in that position, and thus unwittingly gave Seth the looked-for opportunity of drawing the bowie-knife concealed in his boot leg. He knew his mistake only as Seth violently freed his arm, and threw it upward for the blow. He heard the steel slither like a scythe through the hay, and unlocking his hold desperately threw himself on the uplifted arm. The movement saved him. For the released body of Seth slipped rapidly through the opening, upheld for a single instant on the verge by the grasp of the master's two hands on the arm that still held the knife, and then dropped heavily downward. Even then, the hay that had slipped before him would have broken his fall, but his head came in violent contact with some farming implements standing against the wall, and without a cry he was stretched senseless on the ground. The whole occurrence passed so rapidly and so noiselessly that not only did McKinstry's challenge fall upon his already unconscious ears, but the loosened hay which in the master's struggles to recover himself still continued to slide gently from the loft, actually hid him from the eyes of the spectators who sought him a moment afterwards. A mass of hay and wild oats, dislodged apparently by Mrs. McKinstry in securing her defences, was all that met their eyes; even the woman herself was unconscious of the deadly struggle that had taken place above her.

The master staggered to an upright position half choked and half blinded with dust, turgid and bursting with the rush of blood to his head, but clear and collected in mind, and unremorsefully triumphant. Unconscious of the real extent of Seth's catastrophe he groped for and seized his gun, examined the cap and eagerly waited for a renewed attack. "He tried to kill me; he would have killed me; if he comes again I must kill him," he kept repeating to himself. It never occurred to him that this was inconsistent with his previous thought—indeed with the whole tenor of his belief. Perhaps the most peaceful man who has been once put in peril of life by an adversary, who has recognized death threatening him in the eye of his antagonist, is by some strange paradox not likely to hold his own life or the life of his adversary as dearly as before. Everything was silent now. The suspense irritated him, he no longer dreaded but even longed for the shot that would precipitate hostilities. What were they doing? Guided by Seth, were they concerting a fresh attack?

Listening more intently he became aware of a distant shouting, and even more distinctly, of the dull, heavy trampling of hoofs. A sudden angry fear that the McKinstrys had been beaten off and were flying—a fear and anger that now for the first time identified him with their cause—came over him, and he scrambled quickly towards the opening below. But the sound was approaching and with it came a voice.

"Hold on there, sheriff!"

It was the voice of the agent Stacey.

There was a pause of reluctant murmuring. But the warning was enforced by a command from another voice—weak, unheroic, but familiar, "I order this yer to stop—right yer!"

A burst of ironical laughter followed. The voice was Uncle Ben's.

"Stand back! This is no time for foolin'," said the sheriff roughly.

"He's right, Sheriff Briggs," said Stacey's voice hurriedly; "you're acting for HIM; he's the owner of the land."

"What? That Ben Dabney?"

"Yes; he's Daubigny, who bought the title from us."

There was a momentary hush, and then a hurried murmur.

"Which means, gents," rose Uncle Ben's voice persuasively, "that this yer young man, though fair-minded and well-intended, hez bin a leetle too chipper and previous in orderin' out the law. This yer ain't no law matter with ME, boys. It ain't to be settled by law-papers, nor shot-guns and deringers. It's suthin' to be chawed over sociable-like, between drinks. Ef any harm hez bin done, ef anythin's happened, I'm yer to 'demnify the sheriff, and make it comf'ble all round. Yer know me, boys. I'm talkin'. It's me—Dabney, or Daubigny, which ever way you like it."

But in the silence that followed, the passions had not yet evidently cooled. It was broken by the sarcastic drawl of Dick McKinstry: "If them Harrisons don't mind heven had their medders trampled over by a few white men, why"—

"The sheriff ez 'demnified for that," interrupted Uncle Ben hastily.

"'N ef Dick McKinstry don't mind the damage to his pants in crawlin' out o' gunshot in the tall grass"—retorted Joe Harrison.

"I'm yer to settle that, boys," said Uncle Ben cheerfully.

"But who'll settle THIS?" clamored the voice of the older Harrison from behind the barn where he had stumbled in crossing the fallen hay. "Yer's Seth Davis lyin' in the hay with the top of his head busted. Who's to pay for that?"

There was a rush to the spot, and a quick cry of reaction.

"Whose work is this?" demanded the sheriff's voice, with official severity.

The master uttered an instinctive exclamation of defiance, and dropping quickly to the barn floor, would the next moment have opened the door and declared himself, but Mrs. McKinstry, after a single glance at his determined face, suddenly threw herself before him with an imperious gesture of silence. Then her voice rang clearly from the barn:—

"Well, if it's the hound that tried to force his way in yer, I reckon ye kin put that down to ME!"

CHAPTER X

It was known to Indian Spring, the next day, amid great excitement, that a serious fracas had been prevented on the ill-fated boundary by the dramatic appearance of Uncle Ben Dabney, not only as a peacemaker, but as Mr. Daubigny the bona fide purchaser and owner of the land. It was known and accepted with great hilarity that "old marm McKinstry" had defended the barn alone and unaided, with—as variously stated—a pitchfork, an old stable-broom, and a pail of dirty water, against Harrison, his party, and the entire able posse of the Sheriff of Tuolumne County, with no further damage than a scalp wound which the head of Seth Davis received while falling from the loft of the barn from which he had been dislodged by Mrs. McKinstry and the broom aforesaid. It was known with unanimous approbation that the acquisition of the land-title by a hitherto humble citizen of Indian Spring was a triumph of the settlement over foreign interference. But it was not known that the school-master was a participant in the fight, or even present on the spot. At Mrs. McKinstry's suggestion he had remained concealed in the loft until after the withdrawal of both parties and the still unconscious Seth. When Ford had remonstrated, with the remark that Seth would be sure to declare the truth when he recovered his senses, Mrs. McKinstry smiled grimly: "I reckon when he comes to know I was with ye all the time, he'd rather hev it allowed that I licked him than YOU. I don't say he'll let it pass ez far ez you're concerned or won't try to get even with ye, but he won't go round tellin' WHY. However," she added still more grimly, "if you think you're ekul to tellin' the hull story—how ye kem to be yer and that Seth wasn't lyin' arter all when he blurted it out afore 'em—why I sha'n't hinder ye." The master said no more. And indeed for a day or two nothing transpired to show that Seth was not equally reticent.

Nevertheless Mr. Ford was far from being satisfied with the issue of his adventure. His relations with Cressy were known to the mother, and although she had not again alluded to them, she would probably inform her husband. Yet he could not help noticing, with a mingling of unreasoning relief and equally unreasoning distrust, that she exhibited a scornful unconcern in the matter, apart from the singular use to which she had put it. He could hardly count upon McKinstry, with his heavy, blind devotion to Cressy, being as indifferent. On the contrary, he had acquired the impression, without caring to examine it closely, that her father would not be displeased at his marrying Cressy, for it would really amount to that. But here again he was forced to contemplate what he had always avoided, the possible meaning and result of their intimacy. In the reckless, thoughtless, extravagant—yet thus far innocent—indulgence of their mutual passion, he had never spoken of marriage, nor—and it struck him now with the same incongruous mingling of relief and uneasiness—had SHE! Perhaps this might have arisen from some superstitious or sensitive recollection on her part of her previous engagement to Seth, but he remembered now that they had not even exchanged the usual vows of eternal constancy. It may seem strange that, in the half-dozen stolen and rapturous interviews which had taken place between these young lovers, there had been no suggestion of the future, nor any of those glowing projects for a united destiny peculiar to their years and inexperience. They had lived entirely in a blissful present, with no plans beyond their next rendezvous. In that mysterious and sudden absorption of each other, not only the past, but the future seemed to have been forgotten.

These thoughts were passing through his mind the next afternoon to the prejudice of that calm and studious repose which the deserted school-house usually superinduced, and which had been so fondly noted by McKinstry and Uncle Ben. The latter had not arrived for his usual lesson; it was possible that undue attention had been attracted to his movements now that his good fortune was known; and the master was alone save for the occasional swooping incursion of a depredatory jay in search of crumbs from the children's luncheons, who added apparently querulous insult to the larcenous act. He regretted Uncle Ben's absence, as he wanted to know more about his connection with the Harrison attack and his eventual intentions. Ever since the master emerged from the barn and regained his hotel under cover of the darkness, he had heard only the vaguest rumors, and he purposely avoided direct inquiry.

He had been quite prepared for Cressy's absence from school that morning—indeed in his present vacillating mood he had felt that her presence would have been irksome and embarrassing; but it struck him suddenly and unpleasantly that her easy desertion of him at that critical moment in the barn had not since been followed by the least sign of anxiety to know the result of her mother's interference. What did she imagine had transpired between Mrs. McKinstry and himself? Had she confidently expected her mother's prompt acceptance of the situation and a reconciliation? Was that the reason why she had treated that interruption as lightly as if she were already his recognized betrothed? Had she even calculated upon it? had she—? He stopped, his cheek glowing from irritation under the suspicion, and shame at the disloyalty of entertaining it.

Opening his desk, he began to arrange his papers mechanically, when he discovered, with a slight feeling of
annoyance, that he had placed Cressy's bouquet—now dried
and withered—in the same pigeon-hole with the mysterious
letters with which he had so often communed in former days.
He at once separated them with a half bitter smile, yet after a
moment's hesitation, and with his old sense of attempting to
revive a forgotten association, he tried to re-peruse them. But
they did not even restrain his straying thoughts, nor prevent
him from detecting a singular occurrence. The nearly level
sun was, after its old fashion, already hanging the shadowed
tassels of the pine boughs like a garland on the wall. But the
shadow seemed to have suddenly grown larger and more
compact, and he turned, with a quick consciousness of some
interposing figure at the pane. Nothing however was to be
seen. Yet so impressed had he been that he walked to the
door and stepped from the porch to discover the intruder.
The clearing was deserted, there was a slight rustling in the
adjacent laurels, but no human being was visible. Nevertheless the old feeling of security and isolation which had never
been quite the same since Mr. McKinstry's confession,
seemed now to have fled the sylvan school-house altogether,
and he somewhat angrily closed his desk, locked it, and
determined to go home.

His way lay through the first belt of pines towards the
mining-flat, but to-day from some vague impulse he turned
and followed the ridge. He had not proceeded far when he
perceived Rupert Filgee lounging before him on the trail, and
at a little distance further on his brother Johnny. At the sight
of these two favorite pupils Mr. Ford's heart smote him with
a consciousness that he had of late neglected them, possibly
because Rupert's lofty scorn of the "silly" sex was not as
amusing to him as formerly, and possibly because Johnny's

curiosity had been at times obtrusive. He however quickened his pace and joined Rupert, laying his hand familiarly as of old on his shoulder. To his surprise the boy received his advances with some constraint and awkwardness, glancing uneasily in the direction of Johnny. A sudden idea crossed Mr. Ford's mind.

"Were you looking for me at the schoolroom just now?"

"No, sir."

"You didn't look in at the window to see if I was there?" continued the master.

"No, sir."

The master glanced at Rupert. Truth-telling was a part of Rupert's truculent temper, although, as the boy had often bitterly remarked, it had always "told agin' him."

"All right," said the master, perfectly convinced. "It must have been my fancy; but I thought somebody looked in—or passed by the window."

But here Johnny, who had overheard the dialogue and approached them, suddenly threw himself upon his brother's unoffending legs and commenced to beat and pull them about with unintelligible protests. Rupert, without looking down, said quietly, "Quit that now—I won't, I tell ye," and went through certain automatic movements of dislodging Johnny as if he were a mere impeding puppy.

"What's the matter, Johnny?" said the master, to whom these gyrations were not unfamiliar.

Johnny only replied by a new grip of his brother's trousers.

"Well, sir," said Rupert, slightly recovering his dimples and his readiness, "Johnny, yer, wants me to tell ye something. Ef he wasn't the most original self-cocking, God-forsaken liar in Injin Spring—ef he didn't lie awake in his crib mornin's to invent lies fer the day, I wouldn't mind tellin' ye, and would hev told you before. However, since you ask, and since you think you saw somebody around the school-house, Johnny yer allows that Seth Davis is spyin' round and followin' ye wherever you go, and he dragged me down yer to see it. He says he saw him doggin' ye."

"With a knife and pithtolth," added Johnny's boundless imagination, to the detriment of his limited facts.

Mr. Ford looked keenly from the one to the other, but rather with a suspicion that they were cognizant of his late fracas than belief in the truth of Johnny's statement.

"And what do YOU think of it, Rupert?" he asked carelessly.

"I think, sir," said Rupert, "that allowin'—for onct—that Johnny ain't lying, mebbe it's Cressy McKinstry that Seth's huntin' round, and knowin' that she's always runnin' after you"—he stopped, and reddening with a newborn sense that his fatal truthfulness had led him into a glaring indelicacy towards the master, hurriedly added: "I mean, sir, that mebbe it's Uncle Ben he's jealous of, now that he's got rich enough for Cressy to hev him, and knowin' he comes to school in the afternoon perhaps"—

"'Tain't either!" broke in Johnny promptly. "Theth's over ther beyond the thchool, and Crethy's eatin' ithecream at the bakerth with Uncle Ben."

"Well, suppose she is, Seth don't know it, silly!" answered Rupert, sharply. Then more politely to the master: "That's it!

Seth has seen Uncle Ben gallivanting with Cressy and thinks he's bringing her over yer. Don't you see?"

The master however did not see but one thing. The girl who had only two days ago carelessly left it to him to explain a compromising situation to her mother—this girl who had precipitated him into a frontier fight to the peril of his position and her good name, was calmly eating ices with an available suitor without the least concern of the past! The connection was perhaps illogical, but it was unpleasant. It was the more awkward from the fact that he fancied that not only Rupert's beautiful eyes, but even the infant Johnny's round ones, were fixed upon him with an embarrassed expression of hesitating and foreboding sympathy.

"I think Johnny believes what he says—don't you, Johnny?" he smiled with an assumption of cheerful ease, "but I see no necessity just yet for binding Seth Davis over to keep the peace. Tell me about yourself, Rupe. I hope Uncle Ben doesn't think of changing his young tutor with his good fortune?"

"No, sir," returned Rupert brightening; "he promises to take me to Sacramento with him as his private secretary or confidential clerk, you know, ef—ef"—he hesitated again with very un-Rupert-like caution, "ef things go as he wants 'em." He stopped awkwardly and his brown eyes became clouded. "Like ez not, Mr. Ford, he's only foolin' me—and—HIMSELF." The boy's eyes sought the master's curiously.

"I don't know about that," returned Mr. Ford uneasily, with a certain recollection of Uncle Ben's triumph over his own incredulity; "he surely hasn't shown himself a fool or a boaster so far. I consider your prospect a very fair one, and I wish you joy of it, my boy." He ran his fingers through Rupert's curls in his old caressing fashion, the more tenderly perhaps that he fancied he still saw symptoms of stormy and wet weather in the boy's brown eyes. "Run along home, both of you, and don't worry yourselves about me."

He turned away, but had scarcely proceeded half a dozen yards before he felt a tug at his coat. Looking down he saw the diminutive Johnny. "They'll be comin' home thith way," he said, reaching up in a hoarse confidential whisper.

"Who?"

"Crethy and 'im."

But before the master could make any response to this presumably gratifying information, Johnny had rejoined his brother. The two boys waved their hands towards him with the same diffident and mysterious sympathy that left him hesitating between a smile and a frown. Then he proceeded on his way. Nevertheless, for no other reason than that he felt a sudden distaste to meeting any one, when he reached the point where the trail descended directly to the settlement, he turned into a longer and more solitary detour by the woods.

The sun was already so low that its long rays pierced the forest from beneath, and suffused the dim colonnade of straight pine shafts with a golden haze, while it left the dense intercrossed branches fifty feet above in deeper shadow. Walking in this yellow twilight, with his feet noiselessly treading down the yielding carpet of pine needles, it seemed to the master that he was passing through the woods in a dream. There was no sound but the dull intermittent double knock of the wood-pecker, or the drowsy croak of some early roosting bird; all suggestion of the settlement, with all traces of human contiguity, were left far behind. It was therefore with a strange and nervous sense of being softly hailed by some woodland sprite that he seemed to hear his own name faintly wafted upon the air. He turned quickly; it was Cressy, panting behind him! Even then, in her white closely gathered skirts, her bared head and graceful arching neck bent forward, her flying braids freed from the straw hat which she had swung from her arm so as not to impede her flight, there was so much of the following Maenad about her that he was for an instant startled.

He stopped; she bounded to him, and throwing her arms around his neck with a light laugh, let herself hang for a moment breathless on his breast. Then recovering her speech she said slowly:—

"I started on an Injin trot after you, just as you turned off the trail, but you'd got so far ahead while I was shaking myself clear of Uncle Ben that I had to jist lope the whole way through the woods to catch up." She stopped, and looking up into his troubled face caught his cheeks between her hands, and bringing his knit brows down to the level of her humid blue eyes said, "You haven't kissed me yet. What's the matter?"

"Doesn't it strike you that I might ask that question, considering that it's three days since I've seen you, and that you left me, in a rather awkward position, to explain matters to your mother?" he said coldly. He had formulated the sentence in his mind some moments before, but now that it was uttered, it appeared singularly weak and impotent.

"That's so," she said with a frank laugh, burying her face in his waistcoat. "You see, dandy boy"—his pet name—"I reckoned for that reason we'd better lie low for a day or two. Well," she continued, untying his cravat and retying it again, "how DID you crawl out of it?"

"Do you mean to say your mother did not tell you?" he

asked indignantly.

"Why should she?" returned Cressy lazily. "She never talks to me of these things, honey."

"And you knew nothing about it?"

Cressy shook her head, and then winding one of her long braids around the young man's neck, offered the end of it to his mouth, and on his sternly declining it, took it in her own.

Yet even her ignorance of what had really happened did not account to the master for the indifference of her long silence, and albeit conscious of some inefficiency in his present unheroic attitude, he continued sarcastically, "May I ask WHAT you imagined would happen when you left me?"

"Well," said Cressy confidently, "I reckoned, chile, you could lie as well as the next man, and that, being gifted, you'd sling Maw something new and purty. Why, I ain't got no fancy, but I fixed up something against Paw's questioning ME. I made that conceited Masters promise to swear that HE was in the barn with me. Then I calculated to tell Paw that you came meandering along just before Maw popped in, and that I skedaddled to join Masters. Of course," she added quickly, tightening her hold of the master as he made a sudden attempt at withdrawal, "I didn't let on to Masters WHY I wanted him to promise, or that you were there."

"Cressy," said Ford, irritated beyond measure, "are you mad, or do you think I am?"

The girl's face changed. She cast a half frightened, half questioning glance at his eyes and then around the darkening aisle. "If we're going to quarrel, Jack," she said hurriedly, "don't let's do it BEFORE FOLKS."

"In the name of Heaven," he said, following her eyes indignantly, "what do you mean?"

"I mean," she said, with a slight shiver of resignation and scorn, "if you—oh dear! if IT'S ALL going to be like THEM, let's keep it to ourselves."

He gazed at her in hopeless bewilderment. Did she really mean that she was more frightened at the possible revelation of their disagreement than of their intimacy?

"Come," she continued tenderly, still glancing, however, uneasily around her, "come! We'll be more comfortable in the hollow. It's only a step." Still holding him by her braid she half led, half dragged him away. To the right was one of those sudden depressions in the ground caused by the subsidence of the earth from hidden springs and the uprooting of one or two of the larger trees. When she had forced him down this declivity below the level of the needle-strewn forest floor, she seated him upon a mossy root, and shaking out her skirts in a half childlike, half coquettish way, comfortably seated herself in his lap, with her arm supplementing the clinging braid around his neck.

"Now hark to me, and don't holler so loud," she said turning his face to her questioning eyes. "What's gone of you anyway, nigger boy?" It should be premised that Cressy's terms of endearment were mainly negro-dialectical, reminiscences of her brief babyhood, her slave-nurse, and the only playmates she had ever known.

Still implacable, the master coldly repeated the counts of his indictment against the girl's strange indifference and still stranger entanglements, winding up by setting forth the whole story of his interview with her mother, his forced defence of the barn, Seth's outspoken accusation, and their silent and furious struggle in the loft. But if he had expected that this daughter of a Southwestern fighter would betray any enthusiasm over her lover's participation in one of their characteristic feuds—if he looked for any fond praise for his own prowess, he was bitterly mistaken. She loosened her arm from his neck of her own accord, unwound the braid, and putting her two little hands clasped between her knees, crossed her small feet before her, and, albeit still in his lap, looked the picture of languid dejection.

"Maw ought to have more sense, and you ought to have lit out of the window after me," she said with a lazy sigh. "Fightin' ain't in your line—it's too much like THEM. That Seth's sure to get even with you."

"I can protect myself," he said haughtily. Nevertheless he had a depressing consciousness that his lithe and graceful burden was somewhat in the way of any heroic expression.

"Seth can lick you out of your boots, chile," she said with naive abstraction. Then, as he struggled to secure an upright position, "Don't git riled, honey. Of course you'd let them kill you before YOU'D give in. But that's their best holt—that's their trade! That's all they can do—don't you see? That's where YOU'RE not like THEM—that's why you're not their low down kind! That's why you're my boy—that's why I love you!"

She had thrown her whole weight again upon his shoulders until she had forced him back to his seat. Then, with her locked hands again around his neck, she looked intently into his face. The varying color dropped from her cheeks, her eyes seemed to grow larger, the same look of rapt absorption and possession that had so transfigured her young face at the ball was fixed upon it now. Her lips parted slightly, she seemed to murmur rather than speak:—

"What are these people to us? What are Seth's jealousies, Uncle Ben's and Masters's foolishness, Paw and Maw's quarr'ls and tantrums to you and me, dear? What is it what THEY think, what they reckon, what they plan out, and what they set themselves against—to us? We love each other, we belong to each other, without their help or their hindrance. From the time we first saw each other it was so, and from that time Paw and Maw, and Seth and Masters, and even YOU and ME, dear, had nothing else to do. That was love as I know it; not Seth's sneaking rages, and Uncle Ben's sneaking fooleries, and Masters's sneaking conceit, but only love. And knowing that, I let Seth rage, and Uncle Ben dawdle, and Masters trifle—and for what? To keep them from me and my boy. They were satisfied, and we were happy."

Vague and unreasoning as he knew her speech to be, the rapt and perfect conviction with which it was uttered staggered him.

"But how is this to end, Cressy?" he said passionately.

The abstracted look passed, and the slight color and delicate mobility of her face returned. "To end, dandy boy?" she repeated lazily. "You didn't think of marrying me—did you?"

He blushed, stammered, and said "Yes," albeit with all his past vacillation and his present distrust of her, transparent on his cheek and audible in his voice.

"No, dear," she said quietly, reaching down, untying her little shoe and shaking the dust and pine needles from its recesses, "no! I don't know enough to be a wife to you, just now, and you know it. And I couldn't keep a house fit for you, and you couldn't afford to keep ME without it. And then it would be all known, and it wouldn't be us two, dear, and our lonely meetings any more. And we couldn't be engaged—that would be too much like me and Seth over again. That's what you mean, dandy boy—for you're only a dandy boy, you know, and they don't get married to backwood Southern girls who haven't a nigger to bless themselves with since the war! No," she continued, lifting her proud little head so promptly after Ford had recovered from his surprise as to make the ruse of emptying her shoe perfectly palpable, "no, that's what we've both allowed, dear, all along. And now, honey, it's near time for me to go. Tell me something good—before I go. Tell me that you love me as you used to—tell me how you felt that night at the ball when you first knew we loved each other. But stop—kiss me first—there, once more—for keeps."

CHAPTER XI

When Uncle Ben, or "Benjamin Daubigny, Esq.," as he was already known in the columns of the "Star," accompanied Miss Cressy McKinstry on her way home after the first display of attention and hospitality since his accession to wealth and position, he remained for some moments in a state of bewildered and smiling idiocy. It was true that their meeting was chance and accidental; it was true that Cressy had accepted his attention with lazy amusement; it was true that she had suddenly and audaciously left him on the borders of the McKinstry woods in a way that might have seemed rude and abrupt to any escort less invincibly good-humored than Uncle Ben, but none of these things marred his fatuous felicity. It is even probable that in his gratuitous belief that his timid attentions had been too marked and impulsive, he attributed Cressy's flight to a maidenly coyness that pleasurably increased his admiration for her and his confidence in himself. In his abstraction of enjoyment and in the gathering darkness he ran against a fir-tree very much as he had done while walking with her, and he confusedly apologized to it as he had to her, and by her own appellation. In this way he eventually overran his trail and found himself unexpectedly and apologetically in the clearing before the school-house.

"Ef this ain't the singlerest thing, miss," he said, and then stopped suddenly. A faint noise in the school-house like the sound of splintered wood attracted his attention. The master was evidently there. If he was alone he would speak to him.

He went to the window, looked in, and in an instant his amiable abstraction left him. He crept softly to the door, tried it, and then putting his powerful shoulder against the panel, forced the lock from its fastenings. He entered the room as Seth Davis, frightened but furious, lifted himself from before the master's desk which he had just broken open. He had barely time to conceal something in his pocket and close the lid again before Uncle Ben approached him.

"What mouut ye be doin' here, Seth Davis?" he asked with the slow deliberation which in that locality meant mischief.

"And what mouut YOU be doin' here, Mister Ben Dabney?" said Seth, resuming his effrontery.

"Well," returned Uncle Ben, planting himself in the aisle before his opponent, "I ain't doin' no sheriff's posse business jest now, but I reckon to keep my hand in far enuff to purtect other folks' property," he added, with a significant glance at the broken lock of the desk.

"Ben Dabney," said Seth in snarling expostulation, "I hain't got no quar'll with ye!"

"Then hand me over whatever you took just now from teacher's desk and we'll talk about that afterwards," said Uncle Ben advancing.

"I tell ye I hain't got no quar'll with ye, Uncle Ben," continued Seth, retreating with a malignant sneer; "and when you talk of protectin' other folks' property, mebbe ye'd better protect YOUR OWN—or what ye'd like to call so—instead of quar'llin' with the man that's helpin' ye. I've got yer the proofs that that sneakin' hound of a Yankee school-master that Cress McKinstry's hell bent on, and that the old man and old woman are just chuckin' into her arms, is a lyin', black-hearted, hypocritical seducer"—

"Stop!" said Uncle Ben in a voice that made the crazy casement rattle.

He strode towards Seth Davis, no longer with his habitual careful, hesitating step, but with a tread that seemed to shake the whole school-room. A single dominant clutch of his powerful right hand on the young man's breast forced him backwards into the vacant chair of the master. His usually florid face had grown as gray as the twilight; his menacing form in a moment filled the little room and darkened the windows. Then in some inexplicable reaction his figure slightly drooped, he laid one heavy hand tremblingly on the desk, and with the other affected to wipe his mouth after his old embarrassed fashion.

"What's that you were sayin' o' Cressy?" he said huskily.

"Wot everybody says," said the frightened Seth, gaining a cowardly confidence under his adversary's emotion. "Wot every cub that sets yer under his cantin' teachin', and sees 'em together, knows. It's wot you'd hev knowed ef he and Roop Filgee hadn't played ye fer a softy all the time. And while you've bin hangin' round yer fer a flicker of Cressy's gownd as she prances out o' school, he's bin lyin' low and laffin' at ye, and while he's turned Roop over to keep you here, pretendin' to give ye lessons, he's bin gallivantin' round with her and huggin' and kissin' her in barns and in the brush— and now YOU want to quar'll with me."

He stopped, panting for breath, and stared malignantly in the gray face of his hearer. But Uncle Ben only lifted his heavy hand mildly with an awkward gesture of warning, stepped softly in his old cautious hesitating manner to the open door, closed it, and returned gently:—

"I reckon ye got in through the winder, didn't ye, Seth?" he said, with a labored affectation of unemotional ease, "a kind o' one leg over, and one, two, and then you're in, eh?"

"Never you mind HOW I got in, Ben Dabney," returned Seth, his hostility and insolence increasing with his opponent's evident weakness, "ez long ez I got yer and got, by G-d! what I kem here fer! For whiles all this was goin' on, and whiles the old fool man and old fool woman was swallowin' what they did see and blinkin' at what they didn't, and huggin' themselves that they'd got high-toned kempany fer their darter, that high-toned kempany was playin' THEM too, by G-d! Yes, Sir! that high-toned, cantin' school-teacher was keepin' a married woman in 'Frisco, all the while he was here honey-foglin' with Cressy, and I've got the papers yer to prove it." He tapped his breast-pocket with a coarse laugh and thrust his face forward into the gray shadow of his adversary's.

"An' you sorter spotted their bein' in this yer desk and bursted it?" said Uncle Ben, gravely examining the broken lock in the darkness as if it were the most important feature of the incident.

Seth nodded. "You bet your life. I saw him through the winder only this afternoon lookin over 'em alone, and I reckoned to lay my hands on 'em if I had to bust him or his desk. And I did!" he added with a triumphant chuckle.

"And you did—sure pop!" said Uncle Ben with slow deliberate admiration, passing his heavy hand along the splintered lid. "And you reckon, Seth, that this yer showin' of him up will break off enythin' betwixt him and this yer—this yer Miss—Miss McKinstry?" he continued with labored formality.

"I reckon ef the old fool McKinstry don't shoot him in his tracks thar'll be white men enough in Injin Springs to ride this high-toned, pizenous hypocrit on a rail outer the settlement!"

"That's so!" said Uncle Ben musingly, after a thoughtful pause, in which he still seemed to be more occupied with the broken desk than his companion's remark. Then he went on cautiously: "And ez this thing orter be worked mighty fine, Seth, p'r'aps, on the hull, you'd better let me have them papers."

"What! YOU?" snarled Seth, drawing back with a glance of angry suspicion; "not if I know it!"

"Seth," said Uncle Ben, resting his elbows on the desk confidentially, and speaking with painful and heavy deliberation, "when you first interdoosed this yer subject you elluded to my hevin', so to speak, rights o' preemption and interference with this young lady, and that in your opinion, I wasn't purtectin' them rights. It 'pears to me that, allowin' that to be gospel truth, them ther papers orter be in MY possession—you hevin' so to speak no rights to purtect, bein' off the board with this yer young lady, and bein' moved gin'rally by free and independent cussedness. And ez I sed afore, this sort o' thing havin' to be worked mighty fine, and them papers manniperlated with judgment, I reckon, Seth, if you don't objeck, I'll hev—hev—to trouble you."

Seth started to his feet with a rapid glance at the door, but Uncle Ben had risen again with the same alarming expression of completely filling the darkened school-room, and of shaking the floor beneath him at the slightest movement. Already he fancied he saw Uncle Ben's powerful arm hovering above him ready to descend. It suddenly occurred to him that if he left the execution of his scheme of exposure and vengeance to Uncle Ben, the onus of stealing the letters would fall equally upon their possessor. This advantage seemed more probable than the danger of Uncle Ben's weakly yielding them up to the master. In the latter case he, Seth, could still circulate the report of having seen the letters which Uncle Ben had himself stolen in a fit of jealousy—a hypothesis the more readily accepted from the latter's familiar knowledge of the schoolhouse and his presumed ambitious jealousy of Cressy in his present attitude as a man of position. With affected reluctance and hesitation he put his hand to his breast-pocket.

"Of course," he said, "if you're kalkilatin' to take up the quar'll on YOUR rights, and ez Cressy ain't anythin' more to me, YOU orter hev the proofs. Only don't trust them into that hound's hands. Once he gets 'em again he'll secure a warrant agin you for stealin'. That'll be his game. I'd show 'em to HER first—don't ye see?—and I reckon ef she's old Ma'am McKinstry's darter, she'll make it lively for him."

He handed the letters to the looming figure before him. It seemed to become again a yielding mortal, and said in a hesitating voice, "P'r'aps you'd better make tracks outer this, Seth, and leave me yer to put things to rights and fix up that door and the desk agin to-morrow mornin'. He'd better not know it to onct, and so start a row about bein' broken into."

The proposition seemed to please Seth; he even extended his hand in the darkness. But he met only an irresponsive void. With a slight shrug of his shoulders and a grunting farewell, he felt his way to the door and disappeared. For a few moments it seemed as if Uncle Ben had also deserted the schoolhouse, so profound and quiet was the hush that fell upon it. But as the eye became accustomed to the shadow a grayish bulk appeared to grow out of it over the master's desk and shaped itself into the broad figure of Uncle Ben. Later, when the moon rose and looked in at the window, it saw him as the master had seen him on the first day he had begun his lessons in the school-house, with his face bent forward over the desk and the same look of child-like perplexity and struggle that he had worn at his allotted task. Unheroic, ridiculous, and no doubt blundering and idiotic as then, but still vaguely persistent in his thought, he remained for some moments in this attitude. Then rising and taking advantage of the moonlight that flooded the desk, he set himself to mend the broken lock with a large mechanical clasp-knife he produced from his pocket, and the aid of his workmanlike thumb and finger. Presently he began to whistle softly, at first a little artificially and with relapses of reflective silence. The lock of the desk restored, he secured into position again that part of the door-lock which he had burst off in his entrance. This done, he closed the door gently and once more stepped out into the moonlit clearing. In replacing his knife in his pocket he took out the letters which he had not touched since they were handed to him in the darkness. His first glance at the handwriting caused him to stop. Then still staring at it, he began to move slowly and automatically backwards to the porch. When he reached it he sat down, unfolded the letter, and without attempting to read it, turned its pages over and over with the unfamiliarity of an illiterate man in search of the signature. This when found apparently plunged him again into motionless abstraction. Only once he changed his position to pull up the legs of his trousers, open his knees, and extend the distance between his feet, and then with the unfolded pages carefully laid in the moonlit space thus opened before him, regarded them with dubious speculation. At the end of ten minutes he rose with a sigh of physical and mental relaxation, refolded the letter, put it in his pocket, and made his way to the town.

When he reached the hotel he turned into the bar-room, and observing that it happened to be comparatively deserted, asked for a glass of whiskey. In response to the barkeeper's glance of curiosity—as Uncle Ben seldom drank, and then only as a social function with others—he explained:—

"I reckon straight whiskey is about ez good ez the next thing for blind chills."

The bar-keeper here interposed that in his larger medical experience he had found the exhibition of ginger in combination with gin attended with effect, although it was evident that in his business capacity he regarded Uncle Ben, as a drinker, with distrust.

"Ye ain't seen Mr. Ford hanging round yer lately?" continued Uncle Ben with laborious ease.

The bar-keeper, with his eye still scornfully fixed on his customer, but his hands which were engaged in washing his glasses under the counter giving him the air of humorously communicating with a hidden confederate, had not seen the school-master that afternoon.

Uncle Ben turned away and slowly mounted the staircase to the master's room. After a moment's pause on the landing, which must have been painfully obvious to any one who heard his heavy ascent, he gave two timid raps on the door which were equally ridiculous in contrast with his powerful tread. The door was opened promptly by the master.

"Oh, it's you, is it?" he said shortly. "Come in."

Uncle Ben entered without noticing the somewhat ungracious form of invitation. "It war me," he said, "dropped in, not finding ye downstairs. Let's have a drink."

The master gazed at Uncle Ben, who, owing to his abstracttion, had not yet wiped his mouth of the liquor he had imperfectly swallowed, and was in consequence more redolent of whiskey than a confirmed toper. He rang the bell for the desired refreshment with a slightly cynical smile. He was satisfied that his visitor, like many others of humble position, was succumbing to his good fortune.

"I wanted to see ye, Mr. Ford," he began, taking an unproffered chair and depositing his hat after some hesitation outside the door, "in regard to what I onct told ye about my wife in Mizzouri. P'r'aps you disremember?"

"I remember," returned the master resignedly.

"You know it was that arternoon that fool Stacey sent the sheriff and the Harrisons over to McKinstry's barn."

"Go on!" petulantly said the master, who had his own reasons for not caring to recall it.

"It was that arternoon, you know, that you hadn't time to hark to me—hevin' to go off on an engagement," continued Uncle Ben with protracted deliberation, "and"—

"Yes, yes, I remember," interrupted the master exasperatedly, "and really unless you get on faster, I'll have to leave you again."

"It was that arternoon," said Uncle Ben without heeding him, "when I told you I hadn't any idea what had become o' my wife ez I left in Mizzouri."

"Yes," said the master sharply, "and I told you it was your bounden duty to look for her."

"That's so," said Uncle Ben nodding comfortably, "them's your very words; on'y a leetle more strong than that, ef I don't disremember. Well, I reckon I've got an idee!" The master assumed a sudden expression of interest, but Uncle Ben did not vary his monotonous tone.

"I kem across that idee, so to speak, on the trail. I kem across it in some letters ez was lying wide open in the brush. I picked em up and I've got 'em here."

He slowly took the letters from his pocket with one hand, while he dragged the chair on which he was sitting beside the master. But with a quick flush of indignation Mr. Ford rose and extended his hand.

"These are MY letters, Dabney," he said sternly, "stolen from my desk. Who has dared to do this?"

But Uncle Ben had, as if accidentally, interposed his elbow between the master and Seth's spoils.

"Then it's all right?" he returned deliberately. "I brought 'em here because I thought they might give an idee where my wife was. For them letters is in her own handwrite. You remember ez I told ez how she was a scollard."

The master sat back in his chair white and dumb. Incredible, extraordinary, and utterly unlooked for as was this revelation, he felt instinctively that it was true.

"I couldn't read it myself—ez you know. I didn't keer to ax any one else to read it for me—you kin reckon why, too. And that's why I'm troublin' you to-night, Mr. Ford—ez a friend."

The master with a desperate effort recovered his voice. "It is impossible. The lady who wrote those letters does not bear your name. More than that," he added with hasty irrelevance, "she is so free that she is about to be married, as you might have read. You have made a mistake, the handwriting may be like, but it cannot be really your wife's."

Uncle Ben shook his head slowly. "It's her'n—there's no mistake. When a man, Mr. Ford, hez studied that hand-write—havin', so to speak, knowed it on'y from the OUTSIDE—from seein' it passin' like between friends—that man's chances o' bein' mistook ain't ez great ez the man's who on'y takes in the sense of the words that might b'long to everybody. And her name not bein' the same ez mine, don't foller. Ef she got a divorce she'd take her old gal's name—the name of her fammerly. And that would seem to allow she DID get a divorce. What mowt she hev called herself when she writ this?"

The master saw his opportunity and rose to it with a chivalrous indignation, that for the moment imposed even upon himself. "I decline to answer that question," he said angrily. "I refuse to allow the name of any woman who honors me with her confidence to be dragged into the infamous outrage that has been committed upon me and common decency. And I shall hold the thief and scoundrel— whoever he may be—answerable to myself in the absence of her natural protector."

Uncle Ben surveyed the hero of these glittering generalities with undisguised admiration. He extended his hand to him gravely.

"Shake! Ef another proof was wantin', Mr. Ford, of that bein' my wife's letter," he said, "that high-toned style of yours would settle it. For, ef thar was one thing she DID like, it was that sort of po'try. And one reason why her and me didn't get on, and why I skedaddled, was because it wasn't in my line. Et's all in trainin'! On'y a man ez had the Fourth Reader at his fingers' ends could talk like that. Bein' brought up on Dobell—ez is nowhere—it sorter lets me outer you, ez it did outer HER. But allowin' it ain't the square thing for YOU to mention her name, that wouldn't be nothin' agin' MY doin' it, and callin' her, well—Lou Price in a keerless sort o' way, eh?"

"I decline to answer further," replied the master quickly, although his color had changed at the name. "I decline to say another word on the matter until this mystery is cleared up— until I know who dared to break into my desk and steal my property, and the purpose of this unheard-of outrage. And I demand possession of those letters at once."

Uncle Ben without a word put them in the master's hand, to his slight surprise, and it must be added to his faint discomfiture, nor was it decreased when Uncle Ben added, with grave naivete and a patronizing pressure of his hand on his shoulder,—"In course ez you're taken' it on to yourself, and ez Lou Price ain't got no further call on ME, they orter be yours. Ez to who got 'em outer the desk, I reckon you ain't got no suspicion of any one spyin' round ye—hev ye?"

In an instant the recollection of Seth Davis's face at the window and the corroboration of Rupert's warning flashed across Ford's mind. The hypothesis that Seth had imagined that they were Cressy's letters, and had thrown them down without reading them when he had found out his mistake, seemed natural. For if he had read them he would undoubtedly have kept them to show to Cressy. The complex emotions that had disturbed the master on the discovery of

Uncle Ben's relationship to the writer of the letters were resolving themselves into a furious rage at Seth. But before he dared revenge himself he must be first assured that Seth was ignorant of their contents. He turned to Uncle Ben.

"I have a suspicion, but to make it certain I must ask you for the present to say nothing of this to any one."

Uncle Ben nodded. "And when you hev found out and you're settled in your mind that you kin make my mind easy about this yer Lou Price, ez we'll call her, bein' divorced squarely, and bein', so to speak, in the way o' gettin' married agin, ye might let me know ez a friend. I reckon I won't trouble you any more to-night—onless you and me takes another sociable drink together in the bar. No? Well, then, good-night." He moved slowly towards the door. With his hand on the lock he added: "Ef yer writin' to her agin, you might say ez how you found ME lookin' well and comf'able, and hopin' she's enjyin' the same blessin'. 'So long."

He disappeared, leaving the master in a hopeless collapse of conflicting, and, it is to be feared, not very heroic emotions. The situation, which had begun so dramatically, had become suddenly unromantically ludicrous, without, however, losing any of its embarrassing quality. He was conscious that he occupied the singular position of being more ridiculous than the husband—whose invincible and complacent simplicity stung him like the most exquisite irony. For an instant he was almost goaded into the fury of declaring that he had broken off from the writer of the letters forever, but its inconsistency with the chivalrous attitude he had just taken occurred to him in time to prevent him from becoming doubly absurd. His rage with Seth Davis seemed to him the only feeling left that was genuine and rational, and yet, now that Uncle Ben had gone, even that had a spurious ring. It was necessary for him to lash himself into a fury over the hypothesis that the letters MIGHT have been Cressy's, and desecrated by that scoundrel's touch. Perhaps he had read them and left them to be picked up by others. He looked over them carefully to see if their meaning would, to the ordinary reader, appear obvious and compromising. His eye fell on the first paragraph.

"I should not be quite fair with you, Jack, if I affected to disbelieve in your faith in your love for me and its endurance, but I should be still more unfair if I didn't tell you what I honestly believe, that at your age you are apt to deceive yourself, and, without knowing it, to deceive others. You confess you have not yet decided upon your career, and you are always looking forward so hopefully, dear Jack, for a change in the future, but you are willing to believe that far more serious things than that will suffer no change in the mean time. If we continued as we were, I, who am older than you and have more experience, might learn the misery of seeing you change towards ME as I have changed towards another, and for the same reason. If I were sure I could keep pace with you in your dreams and your ambition, if I were sure that I always knew WHAT they were, we might still be happy—but I am not sure, and I dare not again risk my happiness on an uncertainty. In coming to my present resolution I do not look for happiness, but at least I know I shall not suffer disappointment, nor involve others in it. I confess I am growing too old not to feel the value to a woman—a necessity to her in this country—of security in her present and future position. Another can give me that. And although you may call this a selfish view of our relations, I believe that you will soon—if you do not, even as you read this now—feel the justice of it, and thank me for taking it."

With a smile of scorn he tore up the letter, in what he fondly believed was the bitterness of an outraged trustful nature, forgetting that for many weeks he had scarcely thought of its writer, and that he himself in his conduct had already anticipated its truths.

CHAPTER XII

The master awoke the next morning, albeit after a restless night, with that clarity of conscience and perception which it is to be feared is more often the consequence of youth and a perfect circulation than of any moral conviction or integrity. He argued with himself that as the only party really aggrieved in the incident of the previous night, the right of remedy remained with him solely, and under the benign influence of an early breakfast and the fresh morning air he was inclined to feel less sternly even towards Seth Davis. In any event, he must first carefully weigh the evidence against him, and examine the scene of the outrage closely. For this purpose, he had started for the school-house fully an hour before his usual time. He was even light-hearted enough to recognize the humorous aspect of Uncle Ben's appeal to him, and his own ludicrously paradoxical attitude, and as he at last passed from the dreary flat into the fringe of upland pines, he was smiling. Well for him, perhaps, that he was no more affected by any premonition of the day before him than the lately awakened birds that lightly cut the still sleeping woods around him in their long flashing sabre-curves of flight. A yellow-throat, destined to become the breakfast of a lazy hawk still swinging above the river, was especially moved to such a causeless and idiotic roulade of mirth that the master listening to the foolish bird was fain to whistle too. He presently stopped, however, with a slight embarrassment.

For a few paces before him Cressy had unexpectedly appeared.

She had evidently been watching for him. But not with her usual indolent confidence. There was a strained look of the muscles of her mouth, as of some past repression, and a shaded hollow under her temples beneath the blonde rings of her shorter hair. Her habitually slow, steady eye was troubled, and she cast a furtive glance around her before she searched him with her glance. Without knowing why, yet vaguely fearing that he did, he became still more embarrassed, and in the very egotism of awkwardness, stammered without a further salutation: "A disgraceful thing has happened last night, and I'm up early to find the perpetrator. My desk was broken into, and"—

"I know it," she interrupted, with a half-impatient, half uneasy putting away of the subject with her little hand—"there—don't go all over it again. Paw and Maw have been at me about it all night—ever since those Harrisons in their anxiousness to make up their quarrel, rushed over with the news. I'm tired of it!"

For an instant he was staggered. How much had she learned! With the same awkward indirectness, he said vaguely, "But it might have been YOUR letters, you know?"

"But it wasn't," she said, simply. "It OUGHT to have been. I wish it had"—She stopped, and again regarded him with a strange expression. "Well," she said slowly, "what are you going to do?"

"To find out the scoundrel who has done this," he said firmly, "and punish him as he deserves."

The almost imperceptible shrug that had raised her shoulders gave way as she regarded him with a look of wearied compassion.

"No," she said, gravely, "you cannot. They're too many for you. You must go away, at once."

"Never," he said indignantly. "Even if it were not a cowardice. It would be more—a confession!"

"Not more than they already know," she said wearily. "But, I tell you, you MUST go. I have sneaked out of the house and run here all the way to warn you. If you—you care for me, Jack—you will go."

"I should be a traitor to you if I did," he said quickly. "I shall stay."

"But if—if—Jack—if"—she drew nearer him with a new-found timidity, and then suddenly placed her two hands upon his shoulders: "If—if—Jack—I were to go with you?"

The old rapt, eager look of possession had come back to her face now; her lips were softly parted. Yet even then she seemed to be waiting some reply more potent than that syllabled on the lips of the man before her.

Howbeit that was the only response. "Darling," he said kissing her, "but wouldn't that justify them"—

"Stop," she said suddenly. Then putting her hand over his mouth, she continued with the same half-weary expression: "Don't let us go over all that again either. It is SO tiresome. Listen, dear. You'll do one or two little things for me—won't you, dandy boy? Don't linger long at the school-house after lessons. Go right home! Don't look after these men TO-DAY—to-morrow, Saturday, is your holiday—you know—and you'll have more time. Keep to yourself to-day as much as you can, dear, for twelve hours—until—until—you hear from me, you know. It will be all right then," she added, lifting her eyelids with a sudden odd resemblance to her father's look of drowsy pain, which Ford had never noticed before. "Promise me that, dear, won't you?"

With a mental reservation he promised hurriedly—preoccupied in his wonder why she seemed to avoid his explanation, in his desire to know what had happened, in the pride that had kept him from asking more or volunteering a defence, and in his still haunting sense of having been wronged. Yet he could not help saying as he caught and held her hand:—

"YOU have not doubted me, Cressy? YOU have not allowed this infamous raking up of things that are past and gone to alter your feelings?"

She looked at him abstractedly. "You think it might alter ANYBODY'S feelings, then?"

"Nobody's who really loved another"—he stammered.

"Don't let us talk of it any more," she said suddenly stretching out her arms, lifting them above her head with a wearied gesture, and then letting them fall clasped before her in her old habitual fashion. "It makes my head ache; what with Paw and Maw and the rest of them—I'm sick of it all."

She turned away as Ford drew back coldly and let her hand fall from his arm. She took a few steps forward, stopped, ran back to him again, crushed his face and head in a close embrace, and then seemed to dip like a bird into the tall bracken, and was gone.

The master stood for some moments chagrined and bewildered; it was characteristic of his temperament that he had paid less heed to what she told him than what he IMAGINED had passed between her mother and herself. She was naturally jealous of the letters—he could forgive her for that; she had doubtless been twitted about them, but he could easily explain them to her parents—as he would have done to her. But he was not such a fool as to elope with her at such a moment, without first clearing his character—and knowing more of hers. And it was equally characteristic of him that in his sense of injury he confounded her with the writer of the letters—as sympathizing with his correspondent in her estimate of his character, and was quite carried away with the belief that he was equally wronged by both.

It was not until he reached the schoolhouse that the evidences of last night's outrage for a time distracted his mind from his singular interview. He was struck with the workmanlike manner in which the locks had been restored, and the care that had evidently been taken to remove the more obvious and brutal traces of burglary. This somewhat staggered his theory that Seth Davis was the perpetrator; mechanical skill and thoughtfulness were not among the lout's characteristics. But he was still more disconcerted on pushing back his chair to find a small india-rubber tobacco pouch lying beneath it. The master instantly recognized it: he had seen it a hundred times before—it was Uncle Ben's. It was not there when he had closed the room yesterday afternoon. Either Uncle Ben had been there last night, or had anticipated him this morning. But in the latter case he would scarcely have overlooked his fallen property—that, in the darkness of the night, might have readily escaped detection. His brow darkened with a sudden conviction that it was Uncle Ben who was the real and only offender, and that his simplicity of the previous night was part of his deception. A sickening sense that he had been again duped—but why or to what purpose he hardly dared to think—overcame him. Who among these strange people could he ever again trust? After the fashion of more elevated individuals, he had accepted the respect and kindness of those he believed his inferiors as a natural tribute to his own superiority; any change in THEIR feelings must therefore be hypocrisy or disloyalty; it never occurred to him that HE might have fallen below their standard.

The arrival of the children and the resumption of his duties for a time diverted him. But although the morning's exercise restored the master's self-confidence, it cannot be said to have improved his judgment. Disdaining to question Rupert Filgee, as the possible confidant of Uncle Ben, he answered the curious inquiries of the children as to the broken doorlock with the remark that it was a matter that he should have to bring before the Trustees of the Board, and by the time that school was over and the pupils dismissed he had quite resolved upon this formal disposition of it. In spite of Cressy's warning—rather because of it—in the new attitude he had taken towards her and her friends, he lingered in the school-house until late. He had occupied himself in drawing up a statement of the facts, with an intimation that his continuance in the school would depend upon a rigid investigation of the circumstances, when he was aroused by the clatter of horses' hoofs. The next moment the school-house was surrounded by a dozen men.

He looked up; half of them dismounted and entered the room. The other half remained outside darkening the windows with their motionless figures. Each man carried a gun before him on the saddle; each man wore a rude mask of black cloth partly covering his face.

Although the master was instinctively aware that he was threatened by serious danger, he was far from being impressed by the arms and disguise of his mysterious intruders. On the contrary, the obvious and glaring inconsistency of this cheaply theatrical invasion of the peaceful school-house; of this opposition of menacing figures to the scattered childish primers and text-books that still lay on the desks around him, only extracted from him a half scornful smile as he coolly regarded them. The fearlessness of ignorance is often as unassailable as the most experienced valor, and the awe-inspiring invaders were at first embarrassed and then humanly angry. A lank figure to the right made a forward movement of impotent rage, but was checked by the evident leader of the party.

"Ef he likes to take it that way, there ain't no Regulators law agin it, I reckon," he said, in a voice which the master instantly recognized as Jim Harrison's, "though ez a gin'ral thing they don't usually find it FUN." Then turning to the master he added, "Mister Ford, ef that's the name you go by everywhere, we're wantin' a man about your size."

Ford knew that he was in hopeless peril. He knew that he was physically defenceless and at the mercy of twelve armed and lawless men. But he retained a preternatural clearness of perception, and audacity born of unqualified scorn for his antagonists, with a feminine sharpness of tongue. In a voice which astonished even himself by its contemptuous distinctness, he said: "My name IS Ford, but as I only SUPPOSE your name is Harrison perhaps you'll be fair enough to take that rag from your face and show it to me like a man."

The man removed the mask from his face with a slight laugh.

"Thank you," said Ford. "Now, perhaps you will tell me which one of you gentlemen broke into the school-house, forced the lock of my desk, and stole my papers. If he is here I wish to tell him he is not only a thief, but a cur and a coward, for the letters are a woman's—whom he neither knows nor has the right to know."

If he had hoped to force a personal quarrel and trust his life to the chance of a single antagonist, he was disappointed, for although his unexpected attitude had produced some effect among the group, and even attracted the attention of the men at the windows, Harrison strode deliberately towards him.

"That kin wait," he said; "jest now we propose to take you and your letters and drop 'em and you outer this yer township of Injin Springs. You kin take 'em back to the woman or critter you got 'em of. But we kalkilate you're a little too handy and free in them sorter things to teach school round yer, and we kinder allow we don't keer to hev our gals and boys eddicated up to your high-toned standard. So ef you choose to kem along easy we'll mak' you comf'ble on a hoss we've got waitin' outside, an' escort you across the line. Ef you don't—we'll take you anyway."

The master cast a rapid glance around him. In his quickness of perception he had already noted that the led horse among the cavalcade was fastened by a lariat to one of the riders so that escape by flight was impossible, and that he had not a single weapon to defend himself with or even provoke, in his desperation, the struggle that could forestall ignominy by death. Nothing was left him but his voice, clear and trenchant as he faced them.

"You are twelve to one," he said calmly, "but if there is a single man among you who dare step forward and accuse me of what you only TOGETHER dare do, I will tell him he is a liar and a coward, and stand here ready to make it good against him. You come here as judge and jury condemning me without trial, and confronting me with no accusers; you come here as lawless avengers of your honor, and you dare not give ME the privilege of as lawlessly defending my own."

There was another slight murmur among the men, but the leader moved impatiently forward. "We've had enough o' your preachin': we want YOU," he said roughly. "Come."

"Stop," said a dull voice.

It came from a mute figure which had remained motionless among the others. Every eye was turned upon it as it rose and lazily pushed the cloth from its face.

"Hiram McKinstry!" said the others in mingled tones of astonishment and suspicion.

"That's me!" said McKinstry, coming forward with heavy deliberation. "I joined this yer delegation at the crossroads instead o' my brother, who had the call. I reckon et's all the same—or mebbe better. For I perpose to take this yer gentleman off your hands."

He lifted his slumbrous eyes for the first time to the master, and at the same time put himself between him and Harrison. "I perpose," he continued, "to take him at his word; I perpose ter give him a chance to answer with a gun. And ez I reckon, by all accounts, there's no man yer ez hez a better right than ME, I perpose to be the man to put that question to him in the same way. Et may not suit some gents," he continued slowly, facing an angry exclamation from the lank figure behind him, "ez would prefer to hev eleven men to take up THEIR private quo'lls, but even then I reckon that the man who is the most injured hez the right to the first say and that man's ME."

With a careful deliberation that had a double significance to the malcontents, he handed his own rifle to the master and without looking at him continued: "I reckon, sir, you've seen that afore, but ef it ain't quite to your hand, any of those gents, I kalkilate, will be high-toned enuff to giv you the chyce o' theirs. And there's no need o' trapsin' beyon' the township lines, to fix this yer affair; I perpose to do it in ten minutes in the brush yonder."

Whatever might have been the feelings and intentions of the men around him, the precedence of McKinstry's right to the duello was a principle too deeply rooted in their traditions to deny; if any resistance to it had been contemplated by some of them, the fact that the master was now armed, and that Mr. McKinstry would quickly do battle at his side with a revolver in defence of his rights, checked any expression. They silently drew back as the master and McKinstry slowly passed out of the school-house together, and then followed in their rear. In that interval the master turned to McKinstry and said in a low voice: "I accept your challenge and thank you for it. You have never done me a greater kindness— whatever I have done to YOU—yet I want you to believe that neither now nor THEN—I meant you any harm."

"Ef you mean by that, sir, that ye reckon ye won't return my fire, ye're blind and wrong. For it will do you no good with them," he said with a significant wave of his crippled hand towards the following crowd, "nor me neither."

Firmly resolved, however, that he would not fire at McKinstry, and clinging blindly to this which he believed was the last idea of his foolish life, he continued on without another word until they reached the open strip of chemisal that flanked the clearing.

The rude preliminaries were soon settled. The parties armed with rifles were to fire at the word from a distance of eighty yards, and then approach each other, continuing the fight with revolvers until one or the other fell. The selection of seconds was effected by the elder Harrison acting for McKinstry, and after a moment's delay by the volunteering of the long, lank figure previously noted to act for the master. Preoccupied by other thoughts, Mr. Ford paid little heed to his self-elected supporter, who to the others seemed to be only taking that method of showing his contempt for McKinstry's recent insult. The master received the rifle mechanically from his hand and walked to position. He noticed, however, and remembered afterwards that his second was half hidden by the trunk of a large pine to his right that marked the limit of the ground.

In that supreme moment it must be recorded, albeit against all preconceived theory, that he did NOT review his past life, was NOT illuminated by a flash of remorseful or sentimental memory, and did NOT commend his soul to his Maker, but that he was simply and keenly alive to the very actual present in which he still existed and to his one idea of not firing at his adversary. And if anything could render his conduct more theoretically incorrect it was a certain exalted sense that he was doing quite right and was not only NOT a bad sort of fellow, but one whom his survivors might possibly regret!

"Are you ready, gentlemen? One—two—three—fi . . . !"

The explosions were singularly simultaneous—so remarkable in fact that it seemed to the master that his rifle, fired in the air, had given a DOUBLE report. A light wreath of smoke lay between him and his opponent. He was unhurt—so evidently was his adversary, for the voice rose again.

"Advance! . . . Hallo there! Stop!"

He looked up quickly to see McKinstry stagger and then fall

heavily to the ground.

With an exclamation of horror, the first and only terrible emotion he had felt, he ran to the fallen man, as Harrison reached his side at the same moment.

"For God's sake," he said wildly, throwing himself on his knees beside McKinstry, "what has happened? For I swear to you, I never aimed at you! I fired in the air. Speak! Tell him, you," he turned with a despairing appeal to Harrison, "you must have seen it all—tell him it was not me!"

A half wondering, half incredulous smile passed quickly over Harrison's face. "In course you didn't MEAN it," he said dryly, "but let that slide. Get up and get away from yer, while you kin," he added impatiently, with a significant glance at one or two men who lingered after the sudden and general dispersion of the crowd at McKinstry's fall. "Get—will ye!"

"Never!" said the young man passionately, "until he knows that it was not my hand that fired that shot."

McKinstry painfully struggled to his elbow. "It took me yere," he said with a slow deliberation, as if answering some previous question, and pointing to his hip, "and it kinder let me down when I started forward at the second call."

"But it was not I who did it, McKinstry, I swear it. Hear me! For God's sake, say you believe me."

McKinstry turned his drowsy troubled eyes upon the master as if he were vaguely recalling something. "Stand back thar a minit, will ye," he said to Harrison, with a languid wave of his crippled hand; "I want ter speak to this yer man."

Harrison drew back a few paces and the master sought to

take the wounded man's hand, but he was stopped by a gesture. "Where hev you put Cressy?" McKinstry said slowly.

"I don't understand you," stammered Ford.

"Where are you hidin' her from me?" repeated McKinstry with painful distinctness. "Whar hev you run her to, that you're reckonin' to jine her arter—arter—THIS?"

"I am not hiding her! I am not going to her! I do not know where she is. I have not seen her since we parted early this morning without a word of meeting again," said the master rapidly, yet with a bewildered astonishment that was obvious even to the dulled faculties of his hearer.

"That war true?" asked McKinstry, laying his hand upon the master's shoulder and bringing his dull eyes to the level of the young man's.

"It is the whole truth," said Ford fervently, "and true also that I never raised my hand against you."

McKinstry beckoned to Harrison and the two others who had joined him, and then sank partly back with his hand upon his side, where the slow empurpling of his red shirt showed the slight ooze of a deeply-seated wound.

"You fellers kin take me over to the ranch," he said calmly, "and let him," pointing to Ford, "ride your best hoss fer the doctor. I don't," he continued in grave explanation, "gin'rally use a doctor, but this yer is suthin' outside the old woman's regular gait." He paused, and then drawing the master's head down towards him, he added in his ear, "When I get to hev a look at the size and shape o' this yer ball that's in my hip, I'll—I'll—I'll—be—a—little more kam!" A gleam of dull significance struggled into his eye. The master evidently understood him, for he rose quickly, ran to the horse, mounted him and dashed off for medical assistance, while McKinstry, closing his heavy lids, anticipated this looked-for calm by fainting gently away.

CHAPTER XIII

Of the various sentimental fallacies entertained by adult humanity in regard to childhood, none are more ingeniously inaccurate and gratuitously idiotic than a comfortable belief in its profound ignorance of the events in which it daily moves, and the motives and characters of the people who surround it. Yet even the occasional revelations of an enfant terrible are as nothing compared to the perilous secrets which a discreet infant daily buttons up, or secures with a hook-and-eye, or even fastens with a safety-pin across its gentle bosom. Society can never cease to be grateful for that tact and consideration—qualities more often joined with childish intuition and perception than with matured observation—that they owe to it; and the most accomplished man or woman of the great world might take a lesson from this little audience who receive from their lips the lie they feel too palpable, with round-eyed complacency, or outwardly accept as moral and genuine the hollow sentiment they have overheard rehearsed in private for their benefit.

It was not strange therefore that the little people of the Indian Spring school knew perhaps more of the real relations of Cressy McKinstry to her admirers than the admirers themselves. Not that this knowledge was outspoken—for children rarely gossip in the grown-up sense—or even communicable by words intelligent to the matured intellect. A whisper, a laugh that often seemed vague and unmeaning, conveyed to each other a world of secret significance, and an apparently senseless burst of merriment in which the whole class joined and that the adult critic set down to "animal spirits"—a quality much more rare with children than generally supposed—was only a sympathetic expression of some discovery happily oblivious to older preoccupation. The childish simplicity of Uncle Ben perhaps appealed more strongly to their sympathy, and although, for that very reason, they regarded him with no more respect than they did each other, he was at times carelessly admitted to their confidence. It was especially Rupert Filgee who extended a kind of patronizing protectorate over him—not unmixed with doubts of his sanity, in spite of the promised confidential clerkship he was to receive from his hands.

On the day of the events chronicled in the preceding chapter, Rupert on returning from school was somewhat surprised to find Uncle Ben perched upon the rail-fence before the humble door of the Filgee mansion and evidently awaiting him. Slowly dismounting as Rupert and Johnny approached, he beamed upon the former for some moments with arch and yet affable mystery.

"Roopy, old man, I s'pose ye've got yer duds all ready in yer pack, eh?"

A flush of pleasure passed over the boy's handsome face. He cast, however, a hurried look down on the all-pervading Johnny.

"'Cause ye see we kalkilate to take the down stage to Sacramento at four o'clock," continued Uncle Ben, enjoying Rupert's half sceptical surprise. "Ye enter into office, so to speak, with me at that hour, when the sellery, seventy-five dollars a month and board, ez private and confidential clerk, begins—eh?"

Rupert's dimples deepened in charming, almost feminine, embarrassment. "But dad—?" he stammered.

"Et's all right with HIM. He's agreeable."

"But—?"

Uncle Ben followed Rupert's glance at Johnny, who however appeared to be absorbed in the pattern of Uncle Ben's new trousers.

"That's fixed," he said with a meaning smile. "There's a sort o' bonus we pays down, you know—for a Chinyman to do the odd jobs."

"And teacher—Mr. Ford—did ye tell him?" said Rupert brightening.

Uncle Ben coughed slightly. "He's agreeable, too, I reckon. That is," he wiped his mouth meditatively, "he ez good ez allowed it in gin'ral conversation a week ago, Roop."

A swift shadow of suspicion darkened the boy's brown eyes. "Is anybody else goin' with us?" he said quickly.

"Not this yer trip," replied Uncle Ben complacently. "Ye see, Roop," he continued, drawing him aside with an air of comfortable mystery, "this yer biz'ness b'longs to the private and confidential branch of the office. From informashun we've received"—

"WE?" interrupted Rupert.

"'We,' that's the OFFICE, you know," continued Uncle Ben

with a heavy assumption of business formality, "wot we've received per several hands and consignee—we—that's YOU and ME, Roop—we goes down to Sacramento to inquire into the standin' of a certing party, as per invoice, and ter see—ter see—ter negotiate you know, ter find out if she's married or di-vorced," he concluded quickly, as if abandoning for the moment his business manner in consideration of Rupert's inexperience. "We're to find out her standin', Roop," he began again with a more judicious blending of ease and technicality, "and her contracts, if any, and where she lives and her way o' life, and examine her books and papers ez to marriages and sich, and arbitrate with her gin'rally in conversation—you inside the house and me out on the pavement, ready to be called in if an interview with business principals is desired."

Observing Rupert somewhat perplexed and confused with these technicalities, he tactfully abandoned them for the present, and consulting a pocket-book said, "I've made a memorandum of some pints that we'll talk over on the journey," again charged Rupert to be punctually at the stage office with his carpetbag, and cheerfully departed.

When he had disappeared Johnny Filgee, without a single word of explanation, fell upon his brother, and at once began a violent attack of kicks and blows upon his legs and other easily accessible parts of his person, accompanying his assault with unintelligible gasps and actions, finally culminating in a flood of tears and the casting of himself on his back in the dust with the copper-fastened toes of his small boots turning imaginary wheels in the air. Rupert received these characteristic marks of despairing and outraged affection with great forbearance, only saying, "There, now, Johnny, quit that," and eventually bearing him still struggling into the house. Here Johnny, declaring that he would kill any "Chinyman" that offered to dress him, and burn down the house after his brother's infamous desertion of it, Rupert was constrained to mingle a few nervous, excited tears with his brother's outbreak. Whereat Johnny, admitting the alleviation of an orange, a four-bladed knife, and the reversionary interest in much of Rupert's personal property, became more subdued. Sitting there with their arms entwined about each other, the sunlight searching the shiftless desolation of their motherless home, the few cheap play-things they had known lying around them, they beguiled themselves with those charming illusions of their future intentions common to their years—illusions they only half believed themselves and half accepted of each other. Rupert was quite certain that he would return in a few days with a gold watch and a present for Johnny, and Johnny, with a baleful vision of never seeing him again, and a catching breath, magnificently undertook to bring in the wood and build the fire and wash the dishes "all of himself." And then there were a few childish confidences regarding their absent father—then ingenuously playing poker in the Magnolia Saloon—that might have made that public-spirited, genial companion somewhat uncomfortable, and more tears that were half smiling and some brave silences that were wholly pathetic, and then the hour for Rupert's departure all too suddenly arrived. They separated with ostentatious whooping, and then Johnny, suddenly overcome with the dreadfulness of all earthly things, and the hollowness of life generally, instantly resolved to run away!

To do this he prepared himself with a purposeless hatchet, an inconsistent but long-treasured lump of putty and all the sugar that was left in the cracked sugar-bowl. Thus accoutred he sallied forth, first to remove all traces of his hated existence that might be left in his desk at school. If the master were there he would say Rupert had sent him; if he wasn't, he would climb in at the window. The sun was already sinking when he reached the clearing and found a cavalcade of armed men around the building.

Johnny's first conviction was that the master had killed Uncle Ben or Masters, and that the men, taking advantage of the absence of his—Johnny's—big brother, were about to summarily execute him. Observing no struggle from within, his second belief was that the master had been suddenly elected Governor of California and was about to start with a state escort from the school-house, and that he, Johnny, was in time to see the procession. But when the master appeared with McKinstry, followed by part of the crowd afoot, this quick-witted child of the frontier, from his secure outlook in the "brush," gathered enough from their fragmentary speech to guess the serious purport of their errand, and thrill with anticipation and slightly creepy excitement.

A duel! A thing hitherto witnessed only by grown-up men, afterwards swaggering with importance and strange technical bloodthirsty words, and now for the first time reserved for a BOY—and that boy him, Johnny!—to behold in all its fearful completeness! A duel! of which, he, Johnny, meanly abandoned by his brother, was now exalted perhaps to be the only survivor! He could scarcely credit his senses. It was too much!

To creep through the brush while the preliminaries were being settled, reach a certain silver fir on the appointed ground, and with the aid of his now lucky hatchet, climb unseen to its upper boughs, was an exciting and difficult task, but one eventually overcome by his short but energetic legs. Here he could not only see all that occurred, but by a fortunate chance the large pine next to him had been selected as the limit of the ground. The sharp eyes of the boy had long since penetrated the disguises of the remaining masked men, and when the long, lank figure of the master's self-appointed second took up its position beneath the pines in full view of him, although hidden from the spectators, Johnny instantly recognized it to be none other than Seth Davis. The manifest inconsistency of his appearance as Mr. Ford's second with what Johnny knew of his relations to the master was the one thing that firmly fixed the incident in the boy's memory.

The men were already in position. Harrison stepped forward to give the word. Johnny's down-hanging legs tingled with cramp and excitement. Why didn't they begin? What were they waiting for? What if it were interrupted, or—terrible thought—made up at the last moment? Would they "holler" out when they were hit, or stagger round convulsively as they did at the "cirkiss"? Would they all run away afterwards and leave Johnny alone to tell the tale? And—horrible thought!—would any body believe him? Would Rupert? Rupert, had he "on'y knowed this," he wouldn't have gone away.

"One"—

With a child's perfect faith in the invulnerable superiority of his friends, he had not even looked at the master, but only at his destined victim. Yet as the word "two" rang out Johnny's attention was suddenly attracted to the surprising fact that the master's second, Seth Davis, had also drawn a pistol, and from behind his tree was deliberately and stealthily aiming at McKinstry! He understood it all now—he was a friend of the master's. Bully for Seth!

"Three!"

Crack! Z-i-i-p! Crackle! What a funny noise! And yet he was obliged to throw himself flat upon the bough to keep from falling. It seemed to have snapped beneath him and benumbed his right leg. He did not know that the master's bullet, fired in the air, had ranged along the bough, stripping the bark throughout its length, and glancing with half-spent force to inflict a slight flesh wound on his leg!

He was giddy and a little frightened. And he had seen nobody hit, nor nothin'. It was all a humbug! Seth had disappeared. So had the others. There was a faint sound of voices and something like a group in the distance—that was all. It was getting dark, too, and his leg was still asleep, but warm and wet. He would get down. This was very difficult, for his leg would not wake up, and but for the occasional support he got by striking his hatchet in the tree he would have fallen in descending. When he reached the ground his leg began to pain, and looking down he saw that his stocking and shoe were soaked with blood.

His small and dirty handkerchief, a hard wad in his pocket, was insufficient to staunch the flow. With a vague recollection of a certain poultice applied to a boil on his father's neck, he collected a quantity of soft moss and dried yerba buena leaves, and with the aid of his check apron and of one of his torn suspenders tightly wound round the whole mass, achieved a bandage of such elephantine proportions that he could scarcely move with it. In fact, like most imaginative children, he became slightly terrified at his own alarming precautions. Nevertheless, although a word or an outcry from him would have at that moment brought the distant group to his assistance, a certain respect to himself and his brother kept him from uttering even a whimper of weakness.

Yet he found refuge, oddly enough, in a suppressed but bitter denunciation of the other boys of his acquaintance. What was Cal. Harrison doing, while he, Johnny, was alone in the woods, wounded in a grown-up duel—for nothing would convince this doughty infant that he had not been an active participant? Where was Jimmy Snyder that he didn't come to his assistance with the other fellers? Cowards all; they were afraid. Ho, ho! And he, Johnny, wasn't afraid! ho—he didn't mind it! Nevertheless he had to repeat the phrase two or three times until, after repeated struggles to move forward through the brush, he at last sank down exhausted. By this time the distant group had slowly moved away, carrying something between them, and leaving Johnny alone in the fast coming darkness. Yet even this desertion did not affect him as strongly as his implicit belief in the cowardly treachery of his old associates.

It grew darker and darker, until the open theatre of the late conflict appeared enclosed in funereal walls; a cool searching breath of air that seemed to have crept through the bracken and undergrowth like a stealthy animal, lifted the curls on his hot forehead. He grasped his hatchet firmly as against possible wild beasts, and as a medicinal and remedial precaution, took another turn with his suspender around his bandage. It occurred to him then that he would probably die. They would all feel exceedingly sorry and alarmed, and regret having made him wash himself on Saturday night. They would attend his funeral in large numbers in the little graveyard, where a white tombstone inscribed to "John Filgee, fell in a duel at the age of seven," would be awaiting him. He would forgive his brother, his father, and Mr. Ford. Yet even then he vaguely resented a few leaves and twigs dropped by a woodpecker in the tree above him, with a shake of his weak fist and an incoherent declaration that they couldn't "play no babes in the wood on HIM." And then having composed himself he once more turned on his side to die, as became the scion of a heroic race! The free woods, touched by an upspringing wind, waved their dark arms above him, and higher yet a few patient stars silently ranged themselves around his pillow.

But with the rising wind and stars came the swift trampling

of horses' hoofs and the flashing of lanterns, and Doctor Duchesne and the master swept down into the opening.

"It was here," said the master quickly, "but they must have taken him on to his own home. Let us follow."

"Hold on a moment," said the doctor, who had halted before the tree. "What's all this? Why, it's baby Filgee—by thunder!"

In another moment they had both dismounted and were leaning over the half conscious child. Johnny turned his feverishly bright eyes from the lantern to the master and back again.

"What is it, Johnny boy?" asked the master tenderly. "Were you lost?"

With a gleam of feverish exaltation, Johnny rose, albeit wanderingly, to the occasion!

"Hit!" he lisped feebly, "Hit in a doell! at the age of theven."

"What!" asked the bewildered master.

But Doctor Duchesne, after a single swift scrutiny of the boy's face, had unearthed him from his nest of leaves, laid him in his lap, and deftly ripped away the preposterous bandage. "Hold the light here. By Jove! he tells the truth. Who did it, Johnny?"

But Johnny was silent. In an interval of feverish conscious-ness and pain, his perception and memory had been quickened; a suspicion of the real cause of his disaster had dawned upon him—but his childish lips were heroically sealed. The master glanced appealingly at the Doctor.

"Take him before you in the saddle to McKinstry's," said the latter promptly. "I can attend to both."

The master lifted the boy tenderly in his arms. Johnny, stimulated by the prospect of a free ride, became feebly interested in his fellow sufferer.

"Did Theth hit him bad?" he asked.

"Seth?" echoed the master, wildly.

"Yeth. I theed him when he took aim."

The master did not reply, but the next moment Johnny felt himself clasped in his arms in the saddle before him, borne like a whirlwind in the direction of the McKinstry ranch.

CHAPTER XIV

They found the wounded man lying in the front room upon a rudely extemporized couch of bear-skins, he having sternly declined the effeminacy of his wife's bedroom. In the possibility of a fatal termination to his wound, and in obedience to a grim frontier tradition, he had also refused to have his boots removed in order that he might "die with them on," as became his ancestral custom. Johnny was therefore speedily made comfortable in the McKinstry bed, while Dr. Duchesne gave his whole attention to his more serious patient. The master glanced hurriedly around for Mrs. McKinstry. She was not only absent from the room, but there seemed to be no suggestion of her presence in the house. To his greater surprise the hurried inquiry that rose to his lips was checked by a significant warning from the attendant. He sat down beside the now sleeping boy, and awaited the doctor's return with his mind wandering between the condition of the little sufferer and the singular revelation that had momentarily escaped his childish lips. If Johnny had actually seen Seth fire at McKinstry, the latter's mysterious wound was accounted for—but not Seth's motive. The act was so utterly incomprehensible and inconsistent with Seth's avowed hatred of the master that the boy must have been delirious.

He was roused by the entrance of the surgeon. "It's not so

bad as I thought," he said, with a reassuring nod. "It was a mighty close shave between a shattered bone and a severed artery, but we've got the ball, and he'll pull through in a week. By Jove! though—the old fire-eater was more concerned about finding the ball than living or dying! Go in there—he wants to see you. Don't let him talk too much. He's called in a lot of his friends for some reason or other—and there's a regular mass-meeting in there. Go in, and get rid of 'em. I'll look after baby Filgee—though the little chap will be all right again after another dressing."

The master cast a hurried look of relief at the surgeon, and re-entered the front room. It was filled with men whom the master instinctively recognized as his former adversaries. But they gave way before him with a certain rude respect and half abashed sympathy as McKinstry called him to his side. The wounded man grasped his hand. "Lift me up a bit," he whispered. The master assisted him with difficulty to his elbow.

"Gentlemen!" said McKinstry, with a characteristic wave of his crippled hand towards the crowd as he laid the other on the master's shoulder. "Ye heerd me talkin' a minit ago; ye heer me now. This yer young man as we've slipped up on and meskalkilated has told the truth—every time! Ye ken tie to him whenever and wherever ye want to. Ye ain't expected to feel ez I feel, in course, but the man ez goes back on HIM—quo'lls with me. That's all—and thanks for inquiring friends. Ye'll git now, boys, and leave him a minit with me."

The men filed slowly out, a few lingering long enough to shake the master's hand with grave earnestness, or half smiling, half abashed embarrassment. The master received the proffered reconciliation of these men, who but a few hours before would have lynched him with equal sincerity, with cold bewilderment. As the door closed on the last of the party he turned to McKinstry. The wounded man had sunk down again, but was regarding with drowsy satisfaction a leaden bullet he was holding between his finger and thumb.

"This yer shot, Mr. Ford," he said in a slow voice, whose weakness was only indicated by its extreme deliberation, "never kem from the gun I gave ye—and was never fired by you." He paused and then added with his old dull abstraction, "It's a long time since I've run agin anythin' that makes me feel more—kam."

In Mr. McKinstry's weak condition the master did not dare to make Johnny's revelation known to him, and contented himself by simply pressing his hand, but the next moment the wounded man resumed,—

"That ball jest fits Seth's navy revolver—and the hound hes made tracks outer the country."

"But what motive could he have in attacking YOU at such a time?" asked the master.

"He reckoned that either I'd kill you and so he'd got shut of us both in that way, without it being noticed; or if I missed you, the others would hang YOU—ez they kalkilated to—for killing ME! The idea kem to him when he overheard you hintin' you wouldn't return my fire."

A shuddering conviction that McKinstry had divined the real truth passed over the master. In the impulse of the moment he again would have corroborated it by revealing Johnny's story, but a glance at the growing feverishness of the wounded man checked his utterance. "Don't talk of it now," he said hurriedly. "Enough for me to know that you acquit ME. I am here now only to beg you to compose yourself until the doctor comes back—as you seemed to be alone, and

Mrs. McKinstry"—he stopped in awkward embarrassment.

A singular confusion overspread the invalid's face. "She hed steppt out afore this happened, owin' to contrairy opinions betwixt me and her. Ye mout hev noticed, Mr. Ford, that gin'rally she didn't 'pear to cotton to ye! Thar ain't a woman a goin' ez is the ekal of Blair Rawlins' darter in nussin' a man and keeping him in fightin' order, but in matters like things that consarn herself and Cress, I begin to think, Mr. Ford, that somehow, she ain't exakly—kam! Bein' kam yourself, ye'll put any unpleasantness down to that. Wotever you hear from HER, and, for the matter o' that, from her own darter too—for I'm takin' back the foolishness I said to ye over yon about your runnin' off with Cress—you'll remember, Mr. Ford, it warn't from no ill feeling to YOU, in her or Cress— but on'y a want of kam! I mout hev had MY idees about Cress, you mout hev had YOURS, and that fool Dabney mout hev had HIS; but it warn't the old woman's—nor Cressy's—it warn't Blair Rawlins' darter's idea—nor yet HER darter's! And why? For want o' kam! Times I reckon it was left out o' woman's nater. And bein' kam yourself, you understand it, and take it all in."

The old look of drowsy pain had settled so strongly in his red eyes again that the master was fain to put his hand gently over them, and with a faint smile beg him to compose himself to sleep. This he finally did after a whispered suggestion that he himself was feeling "more kam." The master sat for some moments with his hand upon the sleeping man's eyes, and a vague and undefinable sense of loneliness seemed to fall upon him from the empty rafters of the silent and deserted house. The rising wind moaned fitfully around its bleak shell with the despairing sound of far and forever receding voices. So strong was the impression that when the doctor and McKinstry's attending brother re-entered the room, the master still lingered beside the bed with a dazed sensation of abandonment that the doctor's practical reassuring smile could hardly dispel.

"He's doing splendidly now," he said, listening to the sleeper's more regular respiration: "and I'd advise you to go now, Mr. Ford, before he wakes, lest he might be tempted to excite himself by talking to you again. He's really quite out of danger now. Good-night! I'll drop in on you at the hotel when I return."

The master, albeit still confused and bewildered, felt his way to the door and out into the open night. The wind was still despairingly wrestling with the tree-tops, but the far receding voices seemed to be growing fainter in the distance, until, as he passed on, they too seemed to pass away forever.

*****

Monday morning had come again, and the master was at his desk in the school house early, with a still damp and inky copy of the Star fresh from the press before him. The free breath of the pines was blowing in the window, and bringing to his ears the distant voices of his slowly gathering flock, as he read as follows:—

"The perpetrator of the dastardly outrage at the Indian Spring Academy on Thursday last—which, through unfortunate misrepresentation of the facts, led to a premature calling out of several of our most public-spirited citizens, and culmi-nated in a most regrettable encounter between Mr. McKinstry and the accomplished and estimable principal of the school—has, we regret to say, escaped condign punishment by leaving the country with his relations. If, as is seriously whispered, he was also guilty of an unparalleled offence against a chivalrous code which will exclude him in the future from ever seeking redress at the Court of Honor, our citizens will be only too glad to get rid of the contamination of being obliged to arrest him. Those of our readers who know the high character of the two gentlemen who were thus forced into a hostile meeting, will not be surprised to know that the most ample apologies were tendered on both sides, and that the entente cordiale has been thoroughly restored. The bullet—which it is said played a highly important part in the subsequent explanation, proving to have come from a REVOLVER fired by some outsider—has been extracted from Mr. McKinstry's thigh, and he is doing well, with every prospect of a speedy recovery."

Smiling, albeit not uncomplacently, at this valuable contribution to history from an unfettered press, his eye fell upon the next paragraph, perhaps not so complacently:—

"Benjamin Daubigny, Esq., who left town for Sacramento on important business, not entirely unconnected with his new interests in Indian Springs, will, it is rumored, be shortly joined by his wife, who has been enabled by his recent good fortune to leave her old home in the States, and take her proper proud position at his side. Although personally unknown to Indian Springs, Mrs. Daubigny is spoken of as a beautiful and singularly accomplished woman, and it is to be regretted that her husband's interests will compel them to abandon Indian Springs for Sacramento as a future residence. Mr. Daubigny was accompanied by his private secretary Rupert, the eldest son of H. G. Filgee, Esq., who has been a promising graduate of the Indian Spring Academy, and offers a bright example to the youth of this district. We are happy to learn that his younger brother is recovering rapidly from a slight accident received last week through the incautious handling of firearms."

The master, with his eyes upon the paper, remained so long plunged in a reverie that the school-room was quite filled and his little flock was wonderingly regarding him before he recalled himself. He was hurriedly reaching his hand towards the bell when he was attracted by the rising figure of Octavia Dean.

"Please, sir, you didn't ask if we had any news!"

"True—I forgot," said the master smiling. "Well, have you anything to tell us?"

"Yes, sir. Cressy McKinstry has left school."

"Indeed!"

"Yes, sir; she's married."

"Married," repeated the master with an effort, yet conscious of the eyes concentrated upon his colorless face. "Married—and to whom?"

"To Joe Masters, sir, at the Baptist Chapel at Big Bluff, Sunday, an' Marm McKinstry was thar with her."

There was a momentary and breathless pause. Then the voices of his little pupils—those sage and sweet truants from tradition, those gentle but relentless historians of the future—rose around him in shrill chorus—"WHY, WE KNOWED IT ALL ALONG, SIR!"

ABOUT THE AUTHOR

 **Francis Bret Harte** (August 25, 1836–May 6, 1902) was an American author and poet, best remembered for his accounts of pioneering life in California.

Born in Albany, New York, Harte moved to California in 1853, later working there in a number of capacities, including miner, teacher, messenger, and journalist. He spent part of his life in the northern California coast town now known as Arcata, at the time it was just a mining camp on Humboldt Bay.

His first literary efforts, including poetry and prose, appeared in The Californian, an early literary journal edited by Charles Henry Webb. In 1868 he became editor of The Overland Monthly, another new literary magazine, but this one more in tune with the pioneering spirit of excitement in California. His story, "The Luck of Roaring Camp," appeared in the magazine's second edition, propelling Harte to nationwide fame.

As an established literary figure, he was appointed to the position of United States Consul in the town of Krefeld, Germany in 1878 and Glasgow in 1880. In 1885 he settled in London. During the thirty years he spent in Europe, he never abandoned writing, and maintained a prodigious output of stories that retained the freshness of his earlier work. He died in England in 1902.

Choose from Thousands of 1stWorldLibrary Classics By

A. M. Barnard
Ada Leverson
Adolphus William Ward
Aesop
Agatha Christie
Alexander Aaronsohn
Alexander Kielland
Alexandre Dumas
Alfred Gatty
Alfred Ollivant
Alice Duer Miller
Alice Turner Curtis
Alice Dunbar
Allen Chapman
Alleyne Ireland
Ambrose Bierce
Amelia E. Barr
Amory H. Bradford
Andrew Lang
Andrew McFarland Davis
Andy Adams
Angela Brazil
Anna Alice Chapin
Anna Sewell
Annie Besant
Annie Hamilton Donnell
Annie Payson Call
Annie Roe Carr
Annonaymous
Anton Chekhov
Archibald Lee Fletcher
Arnold Bennett
Arthur C. Benson
Arthur Conan Doyle
Arthur M. Winfield
Arthur Ransome
Arthur Schnitzler
Arthur Train
Atticus
B.H. Baden-Powell
B. M. Bower
B. C. Chatterjee
Baroness Emmuska Orczy
Baroness Orczy
Basil King
Bayard Taylor
Ben Macomber
Bertha Muzzy Bower
Bjornstjerne Bjornson

Booth Tarkington
Boyd Cable
Bram Stoker
C. Collodi
C. E. Orr
C. M. Ingleby
Carolyn Wells
Catherine Parr Traill
Charles A. Eastman
Charles Amory Beach
Charles Dickens
Charles Dudley Warner
Charles Farrar Browne
Charles Ives
Charles Kingsley
Charles Klein
Charles Hanson Towne
Charles Lathrop Pack
Charles Romyn Dake
Charles Whibley
Charles Willing Beale
Charlotte M. Braeme
Charlotte M. Yonge
Charlotte Perkins Stetson
Clair W. Hayes
Clarence Day Jr.
Clarence E. Mulford
Clemence Housman
Confucius
Coningsby Dawson
Cornelis DeWitt Wilcox
Cyril Burleigh
D. H. Lawrence
Daniel Defoe
David Garnett
Dinah Craik
Don Carlos Janes
Donald Keyhoe
Dorothy Kilner
Dougan Clark
Douglas Fairbanks
E. Nesbit
E. P. Roe
E. Phillips Oppenheim
E. S. Brooks
Earl Barnes
Edgar Rice Burroughs
Edith Van Dyne
Edith Wharton

Edward Everett Hale
Edward J. O'Biren
Edward S. Ellis
Edwin L. Arnold
Eleanor Atkins
Eleanor Hallowell Abbott
Eliot Gregory
Elizabeth Gaskell
Elizabeth McCracken
Elizabeth Von Arnim
Ellem Key
Emerson Hough
Emilie F. Carlen
Emily Bronte
Emily Dickinson
Enid Bagnold
Enilor Macartney Lane
Erasmus W. Jones
Ernie Howard Pie
Ethel May Dell
Ethel Turner
Ethel Watts Mumford
Eugene Sue
Eugenie Foa
Eugene Wood
Eustace Hale Ball
Evelyn Everett-green
Everard Cotes
F. H. Cheley
F. J. Cross
F. Marion Crawford
Fannie E. Newberry
Federick Austin Ogg
Ferdinand Ossendowski
Fergus Hume
Florence A. Kilpatrick
Fremont B. Deering
Francis Bacon
Francis Darwin
Frances Hodgson Burnett
Frances Parkinson Keyes
Frank Gee Patchin
Frank Harris
Frank Jewett Mather
Frank L. Packard
Frank V. Webster
Frederic Stewart Isham
Frederick Trevor Hill
Frederick Winslow Taylor

Friedrich Kerst
Friedrich Nietzsche
Fyodor Dostoyevsky
G.A. Henty
G.K. Chesterton
Gabrielle E. Jackson
Garrett P. Serviss
Gaston Leroux
George A. Warren
George Ade
Geroge Bernard Shaw
George Cary Eggleston
George Durston
George Ebers
George Eliot
George Gissing
George MacDonald
George Meredith
George Orwell
George Sylvester Viereck
George Tucker
George W. Cable
George Wharton James
Gertrude Atherton
Gordon Casserly
Grace E. King
Grace Gallatin
Grace Greenwood
Grant Allen
Guillermo A. Sherwell
Gulielma Zollinger
Gustav Flaubert
H. A. Cody
H. B. Irving
H.C. Bailey
H. G. Wells
H. H. Munro
H. Irving Hancock
H. R. Naylor
H. Rider Haggard
H. W. C. Davis
Haldeman Julius
Hall Caine
Hamilton Wright Mabie
Hans Christian Andersen
Harold Avery
Harold McGrath
Harriet Beecher Stowe
Harry Castlemon
Harry Coghill
Harry Houidini

Hayden Carruth
Helent Hunt Jackson
Helen Nicolay
Hendrik Conscience
Hendy David Thoreau
Henri Barbusse
Henrik Ibsen
Henry Adams
Henry Ford
Henry Frost
Henry James
Henry Jones Ford
Henry Seton Merriman
Henry W Longfellow
Herbert A. Giles
Herbert Carter
Herbert N. Casson
Herman Hesse
Hildegard G. Frey
Homer
Honore De Balzac
Horace B. Day
Horace Walpole
Horatio Alger Jr.
Howard Pyle
Howard R. Garis
Hugh Lofting
Hugh Walpole
Humphry Ward
Ian Maclaren
Inez Haynes Gillmore
Irving Bacheller
Isabel Cecilia Williams
Isabel Hornibrook
Israel Abrahams
Ivan Turgenev
J.G.Austin
J. Henri Fabre
J. M. Barrie
J. M. Walsh
J. Macdonald Oxley
J. R. Miller
J. S. Fletcher
J. S. Knowles
J. Storer Clouston
J. W. Duffield
Jack London
Jacob Abbott
James Allen
James Andrews
James Baldwin

James Branch Cabell
James DeMille
James Joyce
James Lane Allen
James Lane Allen
James Oliver Curwood
James Oppenheim
James Otis
James R. Driscoll
Jane Abbott
Jane Austen
Jane L. Stewart
Janet Aldridge
Jens Peter Jacobsen
Jerome K. Jerome
Jessie Graham Flower
John Buchan
John Burroughs
John Cournos
John F. Kennedy
John Gay
John Glasworthy
John Habberton
John Joy Bell
John Kendrick Bangs
John Milton
John Philip Sousa
John Taintor Foote
Jonas Lauritz Idemil Lie
Jonathan Swift
Joseph A. Altsheler
Joseph Carey
Joseph Conrad
Joseph E. Badger Jr
Joseph Hergesheimer
Joseph Jacobs
Jules Vernes
Julian Hawthrone
Julie A Lippmann
Justin Huntly McCarthy
Kakuzo Okakura
Karle Wilson Baker
Kate Chopin
Kenneth Grahame
Kenneth McGaffey
Kate Langley Bosher
Kate Langley Bosher
Katherine Cecil Thurston
Katherine Stokes
L. A. Abbot
L. T. Meade

L. Frank Baum
Latta Griswold
Laura Dent Crane
Laura Lee Hope
Laurence Housman
Lawrence Beasley
Leo Tolstoy
Leonid Andreyev
Lewis Carroll
Lewis Sperry Chafer
Lilian Bell
Lloyd Osbourne
Louis Hughes
Louis Joseph Vance
Louis Tracy
Louisa May Alcott
Lucy Fitch Perkins
Lucy Maud Montgomery
Luther Benson
Lydia Miller Middleton
Lyndon Orr
M. Corvus
M. H. Adams
Margaret E. Sangster
Margret Howth
Margaret Vandercook
Margaret W. Hungerford
Margret Penrose
Maria Edgeworth
Maria Thompson Daviess
Mariano Azuela
Marion Polk Angellotti
Mark Overton
Mark Twain
Mary Austin
Mary Catherine Crowley
Mary Cole
Mary Hastings Bradley
Mary Roberts Rinehart
Mary Rowlandson
M. Wollstonecraft Shelley
Maud Lindsay
Max Beerbohm
Myra Kelly
Nathaniel Hawthrone
Nicolo Machiavelli
O. F. Walton
Oscar Wilde

Owen Johnson
P.G. Wodehouse
Paul and Mabel Thorne
Paul G. Tomlinson
Paul Severing
Percy Brebner
Percy Keese Fitzhugh
Peter B. Kyne
Plato
Quincy Allen
R. Derby Holmes
R. L. Stevenson
R. S. Ball
Rabindranath Tagore
Rahul Alvares
Ralph Bonehill
Ralph Henry Barbour
Ralph Victor
Ralph Waldo Emmerson
Rene Descartes
Ray Cummings
Rex Beach
Rex E. Beach
Richard Harding Davis
Richard Jefferies
Richard Le Gallienne
Robert Barr
Robert Frost
Robert Gordon Anderson
Robert L. Drake
Robert Lansing
Robert Lynd
Robert Michael Ballantyne
Robert W. Chambers
Rosa Nouchette Carey
Rudyard Kipling
Saint Augustine
Samuel B. Allison
Samuel Hopkins Adams
Sarah Bernhardt
Sarah C. Hallowell
Selma Lagerlof
Sherwood Anderson
Sigmund Freud
Standish O'Grady
Stanley Weyman
Stella Benson
Stella M. Francis

Stephen Crane
Stewart Edward White
Stijn Streuvels
Swami Abhedananda
Swami Parmananda
T. S. Ackland
T. S. Arthur
The Princess Der Ling
Thomas A. Janvier
Thomas A Kempis
Thomas Anderton
Thomas Bailey Aldrich
Thomas Bulfinch
Thomas De Quincey
Thomas Dixon
Thomas H. Huxley
Thomas Hardy
Thomas More
Thornton W. Burgess
U. S. Grant
Upton Sinclair
Valentine Williams
Various Authors
Vaughan Kester
Victor Appleton
Victor G. Durham
Victoria Cross
Virginia Woolf
Wadsworth Camp
Walter Camp
Walter Scott
Washington Irving
Wilbur Lawton
Wilkie Collins
Willa Cather
Willard F. Baker
William Dean Howells
William le Queux
W. Makepeace Thackeray
William W. Walter
William Shakespeare
Winston Churchill
Yei Theodora Ozaki
Yogi Ramacharaka
Young E. Allison
Zane Grey